# Everything Is Fine.

# Everything Is Fine.

by Ann Dee Ellis

LITTLE, BROWN AND COMPANY
Books for Young Readers
New York   Boston

Little, Brown and Company

Hachette Book Group
237 Park Avenue, New York, NY 10017
Visit our Web site at www.lb-teens.com

First Edition: March 2009

Little, Brown and Company is a division of Hachette Book Group, Inc.
The Little, Brown name and logo are trademarks of Hachette Book Group, Inc.

ISBN 978-0-316-01364-2

10 9 8 7 6 5 4 3 2 1

RRD-C

Printed in the United States of America

To my little Van, who was born with this book.

# Everything Is Fine.

## NORMA

On my street.

A white van drives by. And then a red car and I know the lady in the red car.

Her name is Norma and she is big. BIG.

But I don't look at all her fat. I look at her face. Like when she came over to give Mom a bill that had gotten in her mailbox by mistake and said, "So how are you, young lady?"

I said, "I'm fine." And I smiled.

Then we stood there. I scraped some mud off the metal plate on the door frame with my fingernail. She stood there.

"How's your mother?"

"Okay."

"Really okay?"

"Yeah."

That's when I looked at Norma's face again and she had a gigantic mole that I hadn't really had time to look at closely before. There was a hair in it.

"Does she need anything?"

"Nope."

The hair was long. But not that long because I hadn't noticed it before. And it was blackish brown like Norma's hair-ball head.

"Can I come in and see her?"

*Silence*

No.

No, you cannot see my mom. No, you can't, you fat fat lady with a red car and no cats.

"I don't think so," I said.

And instead of saying, "Oh, that's all right. I'll come over later," Norma put her hand on my cheek.

It took up almost my entire face. "Poor poor thing. You poor dear little thing." Her hand was hot and wet and smelled like Oreos or honey.

I stood there holding very still because I didn't know what to do. Finally she pulled away and said, "You and me are going to be friends."

So I said, "I have to go make a sculpture," and then I slammed the door like on TV.

But I didn't lean against the door after I slammed it like on TV.

## COLBY

Out my window I can see Colby Dean's boat. It's just in their drive-way and it says "Dean Machine" on the side with an orange stripe and it's bigger than their Suburban. Colby isn't outside today but he was yesterday.

I saw him.

He was out in the yard mowing the grass, and once, before Dad was gone, when I got to mow the grass, I ran over a snake.

"It's just a field snake," Colby had said when I showed him.

So I picked it up and threw it at him and he yelled and swore and told me to get away away from him and that I'm a sicko.

He came over later and I had the snake in a box and we got a knife and some matches and some fishing line to do experiments. First we opened the head with the steak knife but it was hard because the knife was old.

"You have to saw it. You can't just push down," Colby said.

"Okay," I said, but I could have just pushed down probably.

So I started to saw but I didn't want to saw too hard because I wanted to see the brain.

I sawed and sawed very carefully and slowly to preserve the brain and Colby was getting mad. "Go faster. This is taking all day."

I almost said for him to do it but we had already had a fight and I didn't want him to go home.

Colby didn't used to be this bossy.

I sawed and sawed and then it opened. The brain wasn't really there. I couldn't find a brain.

"Who cares about the dumb brain?" Colby said.

So then we stuck the fishing line in a needle and we put it through the head and then we put the line through the tail and made a necklace.

We were both kneeling over the snake on the hot cement when Mr. Grobin with the belly and ketchup walked up. "What're you kids doin'?"

The sun was bright behind his head and you couldn't really see his face except for the sweat drips that slowly went into balls and glistened before they fell to the ground. "You kids should know better."

Oh.

"Those snakes keep critters away."

Oh.

"I better not catch you doin' stuff like this again. You hear me?"

Colby nodded his head. I just didn't do anything.

And then he walked away.

"This is stupid," Colby said. And he left.

The snake is on my wall — dried up — and sometimes I wear it as a necklace when I'm putting my clothes away or hiding in the closet or doing anything.

I wish Colby was outside right now.


## MARSHMALLOWS

This morning I ate thirteen marshmallows.

I put them in the microwave first for thirty seconds and watched them.

Then I got them out and they were on a plate and I ate them with chopsticks.

A fly was buzzing around the kitchen.

I tried to catch it with my chopsticks.

That's when the marshmallows got hard again and stuck to the plate.

I put them back in the microwave and then I saw Colby out on the boat with his dad.

I opened the window. "Colby! Colby!"

He kept helping his dad and not saying anything back.

"Colby! Colby!" His dad looked up and said something to him. Colby shook his head and his dad said something else.

The microwave dinged and I heard Mom groan in the next room.

9:15. She needed her pills.

But Colby was getting off his boat and walking over.

I hurried to get the pills and the sorbet out for Mom.

She groaned again and then the fly was back buzzing all over and then it landed right on my face.

I hit it hard but I only got my face.

"Mazeline," I heard my mom say, and then Colby was at my window.

"What?" he said.

"What what?" I said.

"What do you want?"

"Nothing."

"Why were you yelling my name?"

"I wasn't."

"Were too. My dad heard it."

"Oh. I was going to see if you wanted some marshmallows."

He looked in better and I said, "They're in the microwave."

"What kind?"

"Regular."

Then Mom really said it loud. "Mazzy!"

Colby took a step back. "Was that your mom?"

I didn't answer him. Instead I did a karate chop at him but the screen was blocking.

"Mazzy, please!"

I did another karate chop and Colby said really fast, "I'm supposed to see if you want to go to the lake." He wasn't looking at me. He was trying to look for my mom. But no one gets to see my mom.

I said, "Okay."

And then I killed the fly on the wall with a super karate chop.

Colby said to meet him outside in a half hour.

"Okay."

And then he left.

The marshmallows were hard when I got back from Mom's bedroom and I had to throw away the plate.

We only have four plates left.

## MRS. PEET

One lady comes over and her name is Mrs. Peet and she is with Family Services.

I say, "Oh."

"Can I come in?"

"No."

"Why not, honey?"

"Why are you here?" I say, and I almost burp too but I swallow it.

"This is the Roanys, correct?"

"Maybe."

"Okay. Well, I'm just here to check on things. May I come in?"

"No, thanks."

"Come on, honey."

"No."

"Why not?"

"Because we are quarantined."

"What?"

"We have a very contagious virus going through this house and we are not allowed to let anyone in."

Mrs. Peet is not fat like Norma.

She is skinny and has on a tight shirt that shows the tops of her boobs.

I look at them.

"Honey, I need to come in."

"Not today," I say. "Sorry, too dangerous."

She taps her toe and looks at her watch and then she says, "You know what? It's your lucky day because this is obviously going to take more time than I have. I'm leaving now but I'll be here Wednesday at noon." She tucks her clipboard in her big bag and turns around.

I think about saying, "Whatever, booby," but instead I just watch her walk away.

## BUTTS

On *Oprah* there is a show about swimsuits for big butts.

Oprah has a big butt.

I think my butt is regular but I still watch the show.

I like swimming.

## NORMA AND MR. GROBIN

I see the red car again, and this time there is a man in it and that man is named Mr. Grobin who had said he better not see me doing that again to snakes.

Mr. Grobin and Norma drive by, and Norma waves her globs of arm fat out the window.

"Hello, Norma!" I yell, and I do a princess wave back to her.

I feel bad I slammed the door on her that one time.

I don't wave to Mr. Grobin.

I hope they don't have babies.

A baby with that hairy mole would be a very sad baby.


## PAINTING

When Dad left, he told me, "Anything but the art room."

"Leave your Mother's art room alone, Maz. That's the only place that is off limits."

He said he'd only be gone a week, but then it was two weeks and then three. He came home for a day but then he was gone again.

So I say Mom's art room is *on* limits.


One thing about that room is I haven't been in there so it smells dark.

I open the curtains and the windows.

I put all the stuff that was out in the corner and mop the floor with the orange spice cleanser that she would always use.

I put the easels away and I bring in the power fan from the front room.

Then I get out her blue painting, the one with the three of us: me, Olivia, and her.

I get it out and put it in the middle of the back wall instead of the *Munch* print.

Then I watch the painting.


I am going to start my own art studio and do whatever I want.

See?

## THE DEAN MACHINE

This is not my first invitation to ride on the Dean Machine.

This is my second.

"Is your mom okay with this?" Mr. Dean asks.

"Uh-huh," I say, and I take off my shirt.

I am wearing Mom's old bikini. It sags on me but I tied it in back.

Colby starts laughing. Colby's mom looks back from the passenger seat and says, "Colby, please."

I just wear the bikini and sit by Colby on the way to the lake.

"I didn't want you to come," Colby whispers. His face has freckles all over it and his feet stink because he just took off his shoes.

"Why not?"

"Because I could take only one friend and I was going to take Randy."

"Oh."

He stops talking because there are speed bumps and we scream when we go over speed bumps.

I wish there was a cemetery too. You have to hold your breath when you go by cemeteries and then Colby would have to say: NOTHING.

We pick up two people on the way: a man with hair coming out his shirt and a lady.

They sit by me and Colby so we have to share a seat belt because they are big people.

Colby says, "This is disgusting," under his breath. Our arms are touching and our thighs. It's not THAT disgusting. I think he likes it.

The man says to me, "Hi, I'm Henry."

"Oh, sorry, this is Colby's friend Mazzy," Mrs. Dean says, and Henry shakes my hand but it's hard to shake hands because he's squished against me.

The girl is wearing a bikini too but hers isn't saggy. Her boobs are big. They are bigger than Mrs. Peet's.

No one says what her name is.

Colby looks out the window.


At the lake Mrs. Dean buys us snow cones while Mr. Dean and Henry and the bikini girl, who I found out is Mrs. Dean's sister and is named Dixie, buy a permit, and back up the boat.

There's a long line.

I get tiger's blood and Colby gets coconut.

We're walking to the dock with Colby's mom just in front of us when she starts running and we hear Mr. Dean yelling.

Me and Colby start running too.

When we get to the dock, all these people are stopping and watching.

Mr. Dean is in the water with the boat.

He's diving down and then coming back up and swearing and then diving down again.

The Deans' friend Henry is standing on the shore yelling into a cell phone and the Dixie girl is standing in the shade over by a garbage can.

"What's going on?" Mrs. Dean says.

But then we all see what is going on: the boat is sinking.

"Oh my gosh," Mrs. Dean says, and me and Colby just watch.

"Why is it sinking?" I ask Colby. He shrugs.

"Why is it sinking?" I ask Mrs. Dean, but she is running up the dock.

Then I ask a guy who is drinking a Pepsi and he says, "Looks like he forgot to plug it in."

I look at Colby. Colby doesn't look at me.

But I say, "Your dad forgot to plug it in."

The boat is going slowly and people in other boats are still just watching. "Will somebody help him! Will somebody help my husband?" Mrs. Dean is running back down the dock.

Nobody does.

## DIXIE

I don't get how Mrs. Dean could have a sister like Dixie — like someone you'd see in magazines.

Her boyfriend is Henry.

Henry is white with black hair not just on his chest but on his back and coming out his armpits.

Henry talks a lot.

He used to be in Desert Storm and he has a duck pond.

He told us this while we were waiting for the boat police.

"I never killed anybody, though."

Colby says, "You didn't?" all disappointed, and Dixie is chewing on her fingernails. Her bikini is pink with dogs on it. My mom's is black.

"Nope. Didn't have to. They take one look at my natural guns and those Kuwaitis start running for cover." Then he shows us his arms and muscles and kisses them.

Dixie says, "So full of crap," and starts to pick a scab on her elbow.

Me and Colby just look at Henry's natural guns.

They're really big.


## MOM'S SISTER

Mom has a sister who is forty-six.

Mom is thirty-six.

Mom's sister is named Agnes and she has five kids.

She lives in Kansas.

Mom's name is Roxie because she changed it from Luella to Roxie after she became an artist.

She lives in Utah.

She only has one kid now.

That kid is me.


## AGNES

Agnes calls on the phone from Jackson and says: Is your mom okay to talk?

I say: No.

She says: Put her on.

I say: She can't talk.

She says: Put her on.

I hold the cordless to Mom's face and she breathes.

Then I get back on.

Agnes says: Is she mad at me?

I say: No.

She says: Her breath sounds good.

I say: Yes.

She says: We're comin' out real soon to help you two.

I say: Okay.

Then she says: Heard from your dad?

I say: Yes.

And then I hang up.

Agnes will call again in three weeks.

## DIXIE WHO IS MRS. DEAN'S SISTER

It's been four hours and everyone is standing by the tow truck boat thing except me and her because we're in the shade and she says, "So?"

I look at her. "So what?"

"So, is he your boyfriend?"

Even though Dixie seems like she's young, her skin is leathery and looks like a purse or my mom's dancing boots from when she used to dance.

"Who?" I say.

"Who do you think?" she says.

"Henry?" I say.

"Yeah," she says.

"No," I say.

"Why not?" she says.

"I just met him and he's old," I say. "Besides, I thought he was *your* boyfriend."

She shrugs and then lies down on the grass and puts her hand over her eyes. I just stand there. "I meant Colby," she says, and her mouth sort of smiles so I can't tell if she's laughing at me.

The boat is out now and it's dripping. Dixie rolls over onto her stomach and undoes her straps right there on the grass where everyone can see.

I look at her back and I look around and then I say, "Yes. Colby's my boyfriend. So what?"

"How old are you anyway?"

I don't answer.

She doesn't say anything.

I bite my nail and watch her some more.

Then I go to the dock.

Dixie is sort of weird. Not like a real adult.

DIXIE AND ME AT THE DOCK: pencil on paper

## BILL

Besides Mrs. Peet who is trying to be our social worker and Norma who is fat, there is an old friend of Dad's named Bill who does home health care. Dad pays him to come here on the side because Mom needs help and Bill also gets her pills when she runs out.

Bill was Mom's idea, and when Dad left, we hardly needed him because we were fine.

Now we need him bad.

Bill rolls Mom onto her stomach or onto her back.

Lately he has to wash her because she won't get up.

I tell him, "Don't tell Dad how bad she is."

He says okay, but I think he'll tell because he and Dad are golf buddies.

Then I say, "And don't wash her private parts. I do that." I say that because I don't think he should.

At first I did do it.

I washed her private parts but every time I did I felt sad.

I said to her, "Will you please do this yourself?"

I always made a mess with bringing the buckets of water to her bed and trying to get her clean.

"Please, Mom. Just do it yourself."

The bathroom would have puddles all over and she'd just sit there.

So I stopped.

Then Bill found out.

He said, "Mazzy, you been doing your job?"

I was watching a rerun of *Oprah* where she gives everyone a car.

"What?"

"You been washing your mom?"

"Yeah."

"I don't think so."

"Yeah. I have."

"Nope."

"How do you know?"

"Because she smells."

"Oh," I said. And it made me mad because Mom might have heard that.

"What do you want to do? You want me to do it?" he said.

"I don't know," I said.

He was standing in the doorway of the TV room and his hands were on his hips like a lady on *Days of Our Lives*.

Bill shook his head and went back in Mom's room.

I think he washes her private parts now.

I wish Mom would just do it.


## FOOD

When Dad found out he had to stay away longer than he thought, he asked Bill to bring us food. Bill asked someone else to do it.

She sometimes forgets. Her name is Lisa and she smells like hair spray. She's Bill's friend who needed some extra cash.

She's supposed to come every week but sometimes she forgets. I feed Mom what's in the kitchen even though all she really wants is sorbet and Diet Coke.

Once I put SpaghettiOs in the blender and gave it to her like a shake.

She threw it up.

Lisa says, "Sorry sister, about last week. José was out of town and the kids were all over and you know how it gets."

I watch her unload oatmeal and juice and hope she got more marshmallows. "José is working real hard these days but he has to go out of town sometimes to do jobs." She takes out ketchup and buns and hamburger. "Oh, what am I thinking. Those are for us." She puts them back in the bag. "You and your mama doing okay? You look like you doing okay."

She takes out cans of soup and a loaf of Wonder Bread, two cartons of sorbet, and three jars of strawberry jam.

I like her big hoop earrings.

"Okay," she says, "I think that's all. I got a call from you daddy. He cranky sometimes, eh?"

I nod my head.

"Why don't he just do this stuff hisself?"

I stare at her.

"He live around here, don't he?"

I stare at her.

"He the guy on TV?"

Still stare.

"They divorced?"

I lick my teeth.

"I hear they not divorced."

Lick them again.

"What's wrong with your mama anyway?"

I scratch a fly off my face.

"He says I got to bring juices and on time or he won't pay me."

I nod.

"Okay then, I see you next week."

There are no marshmallows and no milk.

I climb on the counter and wash my feet in the sink.


## SPRINKLER

Colby is outside sitting in the Dean Machine and I am outside sitting in our sprinkler.

It is 108 today.

Colby is wearing football pads and his swimsuit and he's sitting at the driver's wheel.

"What are you doing?" I yell.

"Nothing," he says.

"Why are you out here?"

"'Cause I want to be."

"Are you on a football team or something?"

"No."

"Oh." And then I say, "Do you want to sit in the sprinkler with me?"

He looks over.

"It looks stupid."

Lately Colby thinks everything is stupid.

"It isn't," I say back.

"Okay."

He takes off his pads and leaves them in the boat. Then we sit in the sprinkler.

When Colby sits, he has rolls on his stomach. I don't say anything.

Two cars drive by, a convertible yellow one and a dump truck.

Another car goes by and a bike with a man on it. The man is whistling and driving with no hands.

"I can do that," Colby says.

"Oh."

"Yeah. Want to see?"

"Okay."

He gets his bike out from their garage. It has a flat tire.

"The tire is flat," I say.

He looks at it and swears like his dad. "Stupid piece of crap." And then he leaves it in the driveway and comes and sits back in the sprinkler.

"This is the dumbest summer of my freaking life," he says.

I say, "Oh."

He lies down in the sprinkler and I do too.

"The grass is pokey."

"I know."

"Why does your yard looks so nasty?"

I look around. There is hardly any green grass and so many dandelions.

I think it looks pretty.

I tell him.

"I guess," he says. "I guess it does if you like weeds."

We lie in the sprinklers.


ME AND COLBY IN THE SPRINKLERS: charcoal on paper

# WEDNESDAY AT NOON WITH MRS. PEET

Mrs. Peet comes over and says, "Okay, today is the day."

I stare at her through the screen.

"I am with Family Services. You are required to let me in or the police will come over here and make you let me in."

It seems like she's lying so I say, "We're fine."

She says, "That's not what the neighbors think. Let me in."

The neighbors? Which neighbors? Mr. Grobin? Norma? The Deans?

She says, "Mazeline, right? It's okay. I just need to check things out."

I say, "Show me your badge or something."

She sighs and shows me her card.

She looks bad in the picture so I open the door.

"So your mother, she lives here with you?"

"Uh-huh."

"Just the two of you?"

"No. My dad lives here too."

She writes something down and then says, "He does?"

"Uh-huh."

She makes a ticking noise and then says, "How's your mom?"

"Fine. And my dad is fine too."

"Is he here?" She looks up at me. Clearly surprised.

"No."

"Where is he?"

"On a work trip."

She nods. "So I've heard."

I don't say anything because clearly Mrs. Peet knows stuff.

"When will he be back?"

I stare at her then and flare my nostrils. She makes another note on her clipboard.

She moves my Willy Wonka sweatshirt and sits on the couch. I sit on the beanbag.

"Can I talk to your mom?"

"No."

"Why not?"

"She's working."

"Here?"

"Yes."

"What does she do?"

"She's a famous artist."

Mrs. Peet looks at a sheet of paper. "Ahh, yes. That's right. Well, I need to talk to her nonetheless."

Nonetheless. Nonetheless, you are not supposed to be here and you have to get out, you government boob lady.

I pull a hair from my bangs. "You can't talk to her. She's concentrating."

"Mazeline, go get her or I'll get her myself."

I pull another hair and it looks gray. "Does this look gray to you?"

Mrs. Peet stands up and yells, "Mrs. Roany?"

"Ms.," I say.

No one answers back.

"Mrs. Roany," she yells again, and again I say, "It's Ms."

Silence.

"I told you," I say.

Mrs. Peet clears her throat.

That's when I say, "The end," and stand up.

"What are you doing?"

I say again, "The end, and you can go now," and I open the door.

Mrs. Peet says, "Honey, you're not getting rid of me that fast."

She gets up, walks down the hall, and starts looking in rooms without even asking me.

I follow her because she didn't ask me.


Mom is curled up today.

But I did remember Mrs. Peet was coming so at least she has some lipstick and a sweater on.

"Hi, Mrs. Roany."

"It's Ms.," I say.

Mrs. Peet doesn't answer me or anything. Instead she writes on a clipboard and she says, "How long has she been like this?"

I shrug.

"Is she always like this?"

"No."

"Mrs. Roany?" she says again.

"She's tired. She was working for hours before you got here."

Mrs. Peet gives me an old-woman look and says, "Has she been to see any health-care professionals?"

"Bill."

"Who's Bill?"

"He takes care of her. He's a nurse and he comes over all the time."

She writes something down.

"What's wrong with her?"

"Nothing."

"Nothing? What's the diagnosis?"

"Nothing. She's just tired, like I said."

Then she's looking at the clothes on the floor.

"What are all these clothes doing?" she says.

"They're mine," I say.

"Why are they in here?"

I don't say anything. Instead, I look in the mirror and I have red eyes today.

"Hey. You listening to me? Why are your clothes all over this room? Don't you have your own room?"

I put my face real close to the mirror and look at the yellow between my teeth.

Mrs. Peet is silent and looking at me and we're both looking in the mirror at each other but I am also looking at the yellow between my teeth.

Then she says, "Something has to be done around here. I don't care who your father is."

I say, "He's coming home soon. He's going to be here probably tomorrow or the next day." I look at her now. I turn around and look at her. "Everything is fine. He's just gone for a few days."

Mrs. Peet is writing something on her clipboard again and then her pocket starts buzzing.

She looks at her cell. "Mazeline, I have to go but I will be back. I need your father's cell number."

I go back to looking at the yellow in my teeth.

"Mazeline?"

I gave her a number.

"That's your home phone."

"How do you know?"

"Because I've gotten the machine six times."

I sort of smile but then I pick up some floss from under a bag of eye shadows.

"Tell me now, Mazeline."

I think about giving her a fake number but instead I say the real one.

She types it into her phone and then shakes her head. "I guess I should warn you, things are going to change around here. You can't be here alone with her. Your daddy and I are going to have a talk."

My gums start to bleed.

And then she sort of jumps over the clothes in the doorway, like if she walked on them, something bad would happen.

And she's gone.

I slam the door after her and then open it and slam it again.

In the kitchen I pull out some mayonnaise and a spoon.

Out the window I see Mrs. Peet and Mrs. Dean talking outside.

I start to feel hot.

MRS. PEET IN REPOSE: crayons on cardboard

## DAD

I text-message Dad a code word: Government.

This is the first time I have ever texted Dad since he left at the beginning of June.

It's now the beginning of July.

He calls all the time but usually I don't answer.

And I never text.

Until now.

Me and Mom are fine except for when the government says we're not.

## NORMA

Maybe Norma could help.

## MOM

My mom used to travel. Before she met Dad.

She has a painting called *Beachy Head*.

"What's Beachy Head?" I asked once when she was working on it.

"A cliff. A cliff by Brighton," she said. Looking at the painting with a brush in her mouth. "It's windy and beautiful and terrifying."

"Oh," I said.

And then she looked at me. "I went there several times while I was in England. The wind made me feel like I could fly."

I thought about that. My mom flying. "One day I'll take you there," she said. "You have to feel the wind at Beachy Head."

"Okay," I said.

And then we both looked at the painting.


## COLBY AND NORMA

I ask Colby if he knows Norma.

"No."

"You don't? She lives across the street."

"I know. She's lived there forever, duh."

"I thought you said you don't know her."

"I don't."

"Oh."

Then, like she heard us talking, she comes out on her front porch, her fat swinging because she's wearing a tank top.

"Hey!" she yells.

Colby swears under his breath and I see her fat again. She is a fat fat fatty. We're sitting in the sprinklers and Colby says, "This summer sucks so bad."

Norma is walking over and Colby is getting up. "Wait wait wait, young man," Norma calls. "I got something for both of you."

Colby still gets up and goes into his house.

She is breathing hard and her flowered tank is soaking under her armpits.

"Where'd he go?"

"I don't know."

"Oh, well. I have something for just you then."

She holds out a fist.

I wonder if she has a fish in there.

"Do you want it?"

"What is it?"

"Get up and see."

She's standing outside the sprinklers in slippers and her makeup is starting to drip from the sun.

I get up and shake the water off.

"Are you excited?" she asks, holding the fist out as I get to her.

"Umm, hmm."

She starts to open it — one finger at a time, but just when I'm about to see, she clenches it again and starts to laugh.

"I'm just kidding, sugar," she says and opens it all the way.

It isn't a fish.

It's two scrunched-up pieces of orange paper.

"Oh," I say.

"Take them both," she says.

I take them and put them in my shorts pocket.

"Honey, don't you even want to see what's on them?"

I shrug and her mole starts shaking again because she's laughing. "That's fine. That's fine, honey. You are one original girl."

I want to karate chop her but instead she does something I didn't know she was going to do.

She grabs me and hugs me.

I am in her fat fat fatty rolly all around me and it's hot and smells like bread and coconut.

At first I just stand there and let her hug me.

Then I put my arms around her.

They don't even get to her sides, and she says, "Oh my."

Finally, she lets me go and her mascara is down her face.

That's when I decide Norma can fix things.


## DEAN MACHINE

I see a strange man out the window looking with Colby's dad at the Dean Machine.

But I don't see Colby.

I'm holding Mom's sorbet and watching.

He has his shirt off and is looking at his arm while Mr. Dean is talking at him with his hands. He doesn't have guns like Henry's.

Then Mrs. Dean comes out and then Dixie, but this time the bikini is blue with stripes and she's wearing cutoffs.

Dixie looks like she doesn't care about anything.

I don't either.

She kisses the strange man. I guess Henry from Wichita is gone.

I don't see Colby.

They all get in the Suburban and Mom says, "Mazzy?"

It's quiet but I can hear her even quiet.

"Yeah, Mom. I'm coming."

The hum of the swamp cooler maybe didn't let her hear me so I say it louder. "I'm coming."

But I still watch.

Mr. Dean starts the car and the Dean Machine slowly pulls out of the driveway.

That's when Colby comes running out in different swimming trunks that I've never seen.

He's running out and then someone else is behind him.

But it's not Randy.

It's a girl.

## MOM

"So it's a girl I've never seen."

She is sitting up and not looking at me.

"I think it's his girlfriend."

Mom's nightgown is the blue one and it's stuck to her chest from the sweat. I lean over and pull it away and blow.

"Does that feel better?"

She turns her head toward the window and I keep going.

"Do you think it's a girlfriend? Because I don't."

Then I tell her about Norma and the pieces of paper she stuffed in my hand that say: "One Free Frosty from Wendy's." And I tell her how I have two.

"So I could get us both one."

And I could because Wendy's is on Ninth and we live on Sixth.

I tell her how Colby is different now and that school might be bad this year because Katy Buchanan said you have to change classes and there's not enough time to get to your locker because you get a demerit if you're late so you have to carry your books all over and you could get a hernia.

I also say, "The only good thing is I'm going to take art like you, Mom."

She still looks out the window and a sweat drip runs down her neck.

I almost tell her about the paintings I already did but I don't want her to know I'm in her studio.

So instead I tell her about Lisa and José and how things are tight for them — that's why we don't have any marshmallows or anything.

I tell her that Norma is driving around with Mr. Grobin and how her fat is bigger than it was last year after the accident when she was here for three days straight and made that soup that gave Dad diarrhea.

That was the first time I ever really talked to Norma.

I tell her I record Dad's show so she can watch if she feels like it.

I tell her there's a social worker named Mrs. Peet who isn't nice and says things have to change.

I also tell her that if she wants, I can help her get dressed and we could go to the beach.

When I say that, she turns and says one thing: "Quiet."


## ORANGES

Lisa got us three oranges.

I peel one and mash it into orange juice for me and Mom.

Mine tastes good but I think Mom's doesn't.

I put the other two in the black bikini top and go to the mirror.

It looks okay except you can see that they are oranges and not boobs.

They still aren't as big as Dixie's.

## ALOE VERA

I have a sunburn from sitting outside, which on *Oprah* they say is very dangerous.
I put my mom's aloe vera on it.

## THE DEAN MACHINE

When the Dean Machine comes back, there is only Mr. and Mrs. Dean and Colby getting out.
I watch them get out and Colby run toward the house.
Mr. Dean yells, "Get your butt back here!"
Mrs. Dean is getting something out of the hatch and doesn't say anything and Colby is turning around.
Mr. Dean gives him a towel and says something I can't hear.
Colby starts wiping the Dean Machine.
I am wearing the oranges.
I put on one of Dad's old T-shirts over them and go outside.
"Hi."
Colby doesn't say anything. He just keeps wiping.
His dad and mom are carrying bags and coolers into the house.
"Hi, Mazzy," Mrs. Dean says.
"Hi, Mrs. Dean," I say.
And she doesn't say anything about the oranges. Colby hasn't even seen them yet.
"What are you doing?" I ask him.
"Crapping my pants," he says.

But he isn't. He is wiping down the boat.

"Oh," I say.

Then I say, "Who was that girl?"

"What girl?"

"That girl who went with you guys."

He stops wiping but still doesn't look at me. "Nobody."

"Nobody?"

"My girlfriend, I mean," he says.

I swallow and say, "I know."

He looks at me now. "What do you mean, you know?"

"I could tell it was your girlfriend."

"How?"

"By things I know."

"What does that mean?"

"Just how I know things."

He sticks a finger in his ear and then his dad comes out and says, "You can work while you talk to Mazzy, Colby." And Colby starts wiping again.

"What's her name?" I ask.

He wipes and then he says, "Sexy."

"Oh," I say. "Where'd you meet her?"

"She saw me at McDonald's and said I was the hottest guy she'd ever seen and she got my number."

"Oh," I say. I think about giving him the Frosty coupon. But I don't.

Then he says, "What happened to your . . ." and he sort of points to my orange boobs.

"They got big."

"How?"

"Just grew."

"How?"

"I took some pills."

He stops wiping again and looks more closely at the oranges even though they are covered by my T-shirt.

"Do you like them?" I ask.

"No."

"Why not?"

"They look weird."

"They do?"

"Sort of. But . . ."

"But what?"

"Nothing."

"But what?"

"Nothing."

And then I think he is almost going to tell me but his mom comes over and says, "Mazzy, we were so sad you couldn't come on the lake with us today."

She looks really tan and sort of even beautiful.

But she is never as beautiful as my mom.

She used to kind of be my mom's friend.

She's not her friend now.

She keeps talking. "Colby said you had to do some things for your mom."

Colby doesn't look at me or his mom because he didn't even invite me at all.

"Maybe next time?"

"Okay," I say.

Then she says, "Colby's cousin went with us today. Do you remember her? Ruthanne?"

I don't say anything. Instead I stick my oranges out.

She looks at them and sort of smiles. I don't know if she is laughing at me or if she likes them or what she is doing.

Then she says, "I only mention it because Ruthanne used to babysit you and your sister and she wanted me to tell your mom and you how sorry she was."

I don't listen to what she says. Instead I sort of shake the oranges around and flick my hair.

Colby is on the other side of the boat then.

Me and Colby's mom just stand there for a while. Me shaking my oranges. Her smiling and looking at me.

Finally she says, "You know, I could take you out for some girl time. Would you like that?"

I don't know what she means by "girl time."

"Do you think your mom would care?"

I shake the oranges.

"Okay, I'll stop by next week when I get off work and we'll go out."

Then she's gone.

ME BEFORE ORANGES: colored pencils on paper

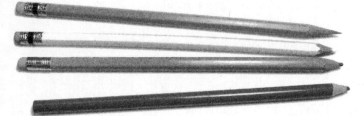

Me after oranges: colored pencils on paper

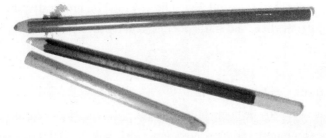

Colby does not have a girlfriend.

## BILL

Bill comes over three times a week, and when he's done, sometimes he watches TV with me.

Or this time, we sit on the chairs outside and he gives me a root beer while he drinks a beer.

"You doing okay?"

"Yeah."

"Really?"

"Yeah."

Then we keep sitting.

Finally I say, "Why doesn't Dad come home?"

I don't know why I say it because I don't really want him to come home. Not really.

Bill sighs. "He'll be home soon, Maz. He calls, doesn't he?"

I don't answer that. Instead I say, "Did you tell him how bad Mom is?"

He drinks some beer and starts peeling skin off his hand.

"Did you?"

"Yeah."

I knew it. I knew he'd tell.

"Then why doesn't he come home?" I ask.

Bill wipes his mouth and then looks at me, "He will, Maz. But this ESPN thing, it's his big break."

I don't say anything because no one cares about ESPN 360. We have to special order the channel and we don't even get a discount.

We keep sitting.

On the chairs me and Bill watch the cars go by and then we watch a lady with a stroller with two kids in it and two kids walking behind her.

"That's a crapload of kids," Bill says.

I don't say anything because I'm drinking my root beer.

Bill looks at me. "That's a crapload, eh?"

"Uh-huh," I say, and it feels like the root beer is going up my nose. I cough.

"Ever want some of those?" Bill asks.

"What?"

"Kids?" Bill says.

"Huh?"

"I mean when you grow up."

I watch the lady and she yells at the kids, and the two in the back are both holding sticks and poking her.

I wonder how old the babies in the stroller are.

"So?" Bill says.

I drink a big drink of root beer and then I say, "Beer is bad for you."

Then we don't talk anymore.

I don't like Bill so much.


## DAD

I can't decide if I want Dad to come home or not.

I usually just want to watch TV.

But then Mrs. Peet came over and things had to change so I had to text him "Government."


That night he calls my pink phone.

I don't answer it the first time. Instead I watch *Survivor.*

The second time he calls it's during a commercial so I answer it.

He says: You picked up.

I don't say anything.

He says: You watching TV, Mazzy?

I say: No.

He says: What are you doing, then?

I say: Making eggplant parmesan for me and Mom.

He's silent for awhile and I turn down the TV then.

Then he says: So what's happening?

I say: Nothing.

He says: Nothing?

I say: Yep.

He says: What about the text?

*Survivor*'s back on so I hang up.

He doesn't call back for thirty-two minutes, and when he does call back, he says: Mazzy, tell me what's going on and don't hang up. Is your show over?

I don't say anything.

He says: What's going on, baby girl?

So then I tell him: There's a lady with big boobs coming around named Mrs. Peet who is from the government because a neighbor called.

Dad says: Crap.

Then he says: I already told her everything is fine.

Then I say: I told her that too. She came in even though I said things were fine and you were just gone on a business trip and Mom is fine and everything, but when she was here, Mom was tired and in bed so she thinks things are bad even though they aren't and she says she doesn't care who you are and that things have to change.

Dad sighs.

I keep going: She says things have to change and I can't live here alone with Mom.

He's still quiet.

I said things were fine and that everything was fine but she said she was going to talk to you and she doesn't care who you are and things were going to change.

She said she doesn't care who I am?

Uh-huh.

Okay.

Okay what?

Okay.

I'm not sure what he means.

I say: Dad, what do you mean, okay?

He says: I mean she's right.

His voice is deep and he sounds not like himself. Not like on TV.

I say: No. No, she's not. Things are fine. Mom's doing really good.

Come on, Mazzy.

What?

Mom's not doing good.

Yes, she is. She just did a painting the other day.

He breathes heavy and then he says: Mazzy, what's been going on was never permanent. You know that. Bill told me Mom is getting worse.

I hate Bill.

So you're coming home?

He's silent again.

Are you?

Mazzy, it's complicated. We'll work something out.

What about Mom?

Mom's going to be fine.

So you're coming home to take care of her?

Silent.

Are you going to put her someplace? We're fine, Dad. We're both fine. You can stay.

Silent.

So I hang up.


He calls back and I let it ring.

He calls back again and I let it ring.

He calls back again and I finally answer.

He says: Mazzy, I am going to say one more thing and then you can hang up.

I pick my toenail and lie on the couch.

He says: Your mom and I love you very —

But then I hang up again.

A rerun of *Judge Judy* is on.

## PADS

Colby wears football pads all the time now.

"Why are you wearing those?"

He ignores me but he's mowing the lawn so maybe he can't hear me.

I get up out of the sprinklers and go by him. "Why are you wearing football pads?"

But he mows right past me.

It used to be that Colby told me stuff like if he was on the football team.

Now he just mows right past me.

So I follow him.

Back and forth and back and forth and back and forth.

Sometimes I march, sometimes I walk slow, but I follow him around the whole yard and he acts like he doesn't see me.

Finally he turns it off and starts pushing it to the garage.

"I know you know I'm here."

The pads are wet from his sweat.

He keeps pushing and doesn't say anything.

So then I don't say anything. I just watch him put the lawn mower away.

Then he gets out two brooms and hands me one.

I sweep the driveway and around the Dean Machine.

He sweeps the front walk.

Afterward he says, "You are a freak," and goes inside.

He doesn't mean it.

I look over and Norma is in her yard.

She waves.

I wave back.

Then I sit in the sprinklers.

COLBY WITH HIS FOOTBALL PADS: chalk on paper

## HAIR

In the mornings, after her sorbet and pills, I sometimes do Mom's hair.

Her hair was short when she first got in bed but now it's longer.

And it doesn't shine.

So I comb it and comb it and comb it and sometimes I put clips in it or bows or once I put a hat on her.

She pulled it off.

I said: It's pretty.

She just lay there.

I said: Come on, Mom. Get up.

She kept lying with her eyes closed even though I know she could hear me. I knew she could get up and comb her own hair and wash her own privates and get her own sorbet.

But she wouldn't.

I said: Either get up or you have to wear the hat.

She didn't get up so I put the hat back on.

She pulled it off.

I put it on again.

She pulled it off.

I put it on again.

She pulled it off and threw it.


You should have seen my mom before.

She was not like this.




## NORMA

Norma is outside and her butt is in the air.

I see her because I'm outside sitting in the sprinklers and Colby is sitting in the Dean Machine.

He doesn't feel like sitting in the sprinklers with me.

I yell, "Norma, what are you doing?"

She doesn't answer and I wonder if she has so much fat in her ears that it's hard to hear.

I yell again. "Norma!"

Nothing.

"Norma! Norma! Norma!"

She turns and sees me and I wave.

Instead of getting up she just plops down on the ground and yells, "Come over here."

I decide to go over there because I want to.

Today Norma is wearing yellow stretch pants and a purple T-shirt that says: "The Objects Beneath This Shirt Are Larger Than They Appear."

That means they are very large. Larger than Mom's, Mrs. Peet's, and even Dixie's.

When I get there she says, "How you doing, honey?" She's covered in mud.

It's even in her fake fingernails.

"Fine. What are you doing?"

"Pulling weeds. Wanna help?"

I turn and look at Colby, who is watching us from the Dean Machine.

"Sure," I say, and she tells me which to pull and which not to pull.

As we're working she is breathing very loud, and then she starts humming this song that I know but I couldn't remember what it was from.

"What's that from?" I ask, and my knees are all wet and muddy now, but I like how it feels.

"What, hon?" she says.

"That song."

"Oh, that's from TV. Fred Meyer commercial."

"Oh yeah," I say. Then I start humming it too.

When we've been pulling the weeds for so long and the back of my neck feels hot so I think it might be sunburned, which is not good, Norma says, "Wait here," and she goes in the house.

I wait and I just sit there.

I look at Colby, who is sitting on the front of the boat now. He acts like he's not looking at me but I know he is, and I say, "Colby."

He adjusts his glasses and looks down the road — not at me.

"Colby," I say, louder.

He starts looking at something on his arm.

That's when Norma brings out three big lemonades on a fancy metal tray plus a bag of Chips Ahoy.

Now Colby is looking.

Norma says, "Come sit over here."

And I go sit with her at her white table that's on her front porch and she gives me some wipes for my hands and then we eat.

Colby jumps off the Dean Machine and starts digging something in his front yard.

We watch.

"Cute boy," Norma says.

I say, "Uh-huh."

Then I say, "Are you kissing Mr. Grobin?"

"No," she says.

I say "Oh."

Then she says, "You kissing that boy?"

"No," I say.

"Oh," she says.

Then I say, "Did you get that other lemonade for him?"

"No," she says.

"Good," I say.

We watch him some more. He's digging and digging and not looking over here.

Then Norma says, "Heard from your dad?"

And that's when I remember the phone call, and I also remember that I was going to have Norma help even before the phone call, so I say, "No. I haven't heard from him."

She nods.

"Have you heard from your dad?" I ask her just to be fair.

Norma pops a cookie in her mouth and looks at me. "Yes. But he's dead."

I think about that for awhile and I like that she said it.

Then I say, "Can you help me and my mom?"

"Probably," she says.

And then we don't talk for four minutes.

Norma would never call the government on us.

NORMA IN A TANK TOP: oils on canvas

## SUV

We used to have a black Range Rover.

That was back when there were flowers in the yard and Dad put in a new sprinkler system.

One time last fall, Mom got out of bed in the middle of the night.

I didn't hear her.

Dad didn't hear her.

No one heard her.

Until she did it.

She took Dad's softball bat — the aluminum one he uses for batting practice — she took it out of the shed from the backyard.

Then she went to the carport, and me and Dad, we still didn't know because we were asleep.

But then, we woke up.

We woke up because it was so loud — smashing and crashing and breaking and screaming, and it filled the whole neighborhood because we only have a carport.

Dad was always going to build a garage but he hadn't done it yet so lights were on all over the neighborhood, and the Deans and Norma and Mr. Grobin and the new family and even Mrs. Cronk, who is dead now because she was old, everyone came out in their pajamas.

We ran outside and Dad tried to stop her.

I just stood there.

And she wouldn't stop.

"I hate you. I hate you. I hate you. I hate you." She was saying it over and over again and the bat made dents and smashed the windshield and the lights and the grill and all over. Dad tried to get to her, but she said, "You get away from me. You get the hell away from me."

And she held the bat like she was going to hit him.

I put my hands over my ears and just stood there.

Mrs. Dean said, "Roxie, it's okay." And she was standing behind Dad and her hair was in curlers. "Roxie, put the bat down." Mrs. Dean always got involved.

Dad was still trying to get close but my mom wouldn't let him.

"I hate you." She said it this time to Dad, loud. "I hate you" — that was to Mrs. Dean. "I hate you," she said to the air, even louder. And then — Dad says she didn't mean it but I know and she knows she did — she looked at me and she said, "And I hate you." When she said it, she said it soft and she was crying.

I took a breath and looked at her. My mom and her eyes.

And then she was doing it again, hitting and hitting and hitting the car.

Dad got her then. He put his arms around her and Mr. Dean took the bat.

Mom was sobbing and a police car pulled up and the rest I don't know.

I don't know because I went inside and I got in the closet.

A tow truck took the car the next day.

I said, "Where are they taking it?"

He said, "To auction. We're not keeping that car anymore."

I said, "Oh."

## MRS. DEAN

Mrs. Dean comes out of her house on Monday in yoga pants and a tight T-shirt.

"Go get dressed, Mazzy," she says.

I am sitting in the sprinklers. "For what?"

"I told you we were going to have a little girl time."

Her hair is pulled in a tight ponytail and I like the headband she has on.

"I can't go," I say.

"Why not?"

"I have to work around the house."

She just stands there and I just sit there.

"Mazzy, go get dressed."

It is weird to have Mrs. Dean talk to me like that.

"I am dressed."

She starts tapping her toe like she does sometimes with Colby.

I look down at the black bikini top without the oranges and my cutoffs.

"Why can't I wear these?"

"Because we're going to a yoga class and then we're going to run some errands. You can't wear cutoffs to yoga, plus you're soaking wet."

"Why not?"

"Why not what?"

"Why can't I wear cutoffs to yoga?"

She shifts her weight and she looks different — not so much makeup.

"Because they don't stretch. You have to stretch in yoga."

"Oh," I say.

"Go," she says.

"I can't."

"Why not?"

"Because my mom said I couldn't."

Mrs. Dean looks at the house.

"Did she really say that?"

I shrug.

"Go get changed, Mazzy. Your mom would want you to go. She just doesn't know it."

I start to get up but then I say, "Is Colby coming?"

"No. He has to fix the bathroom with his dad. Now get going. We have to pick up Dixie and we're going to be late."

Dixie.

Dixie is coming and not just Mrs. Dean.

I do a karate chop at Mrs. Dean and run inside.

## CLOTHES

I keep all my clothes in Mom's room so that she can see what I wear.

She likes to see and tell me if I look okay.

Sometimes I wear her clothes and she almost says, "Oh, that looks good, baby." Or "Umm, that's a bit too tight."

We used to go shopping before.

Mom was a good shopper because she was so classy.

And we would not just go to the Gap or Old Navy like other girls in my class.

We went to boutiques and outdoor markets and places other people would never know.

Me and Mom and Olivia.

She even bought Dad clothes like the pink shirt he wore to the funeral with his olive silk tie.

We found the shirt at a shop called Soel, and Mom was laughing. "Do you think Daddy would like this?"

I was holding Olivia and Mom was going through a stack of clothes.

"Can you imagine him in a pink shirt?"

I couldn't but I knew he would wear it. He wore anything Mom bought and he won best dressed at the station three years in a row.

"What do you think, Maz?"

"I don't know. Probably."

She pulled her hair back and picked through other shirts and I stood mostly against the wall so people could get past me.

I liked to watch Mom and her neck and how she held her body.

Olivia wouldn't fuss when we were at stores, either. She knew.

The two of us were watching the most beautiful person in the world.

"What about this one?" She held up a striped oxford.

"I like it."

"No, too boring," she said, and picked up the pink again.

I should have thought it was too boring. Way too boring.

Olivia fell asleep against my chest, so I just stood there and watched her.

My mom with her neck and her eyes and her smile.

I want to be like her someday.

Just like her.

I still want to even if I have to be in bed.

Now I dress in her room.

I have all my clothes in there, plus I have hers.

I used to try to keep it organized in stacks and rows and boxes, but there were too many clothes and Dad still has most of his stuff there.

So there are just piles and piles.

Her lotions on the vanity.

Her purses hung on the doorknob.

Her shoes strewn across the floor.

I have everything all in there — in case she wants to help me.

## VAMPIRES

Colby tells me he's only attracted to vampires.

"You are?"

"Yeah."

"Why?"

"Because they want to suck blood."

"So."

"So that's sexy."

"Like your girlfriend Sexy?"

And Colby looks mad because he knows I know his girlfriend is really his cousin Ruthanne who used to babysit me.

## ME AND MRS. DEAN

When I am finally ready, Mrs. Dean is sitting in her car in the driveway. I'm wearing my mom's black leggings and one of my dad's T-shirts plus the oranges.

"Mazzy, you can't wear those."

"What?"

"Well, you can't wear that shirt and you can't wear whatever is underneath the shirt."

I look at her.

She looks at me.

She's not my mom.

"Don't you have a tank top or a T-shirt that fits?"

"No."

She sighs and says, "Okay, get in."

I get in her car, which is a Honda Civic with a spoiler.

When the Deans first brought the car home, they invited us to come look at it.

Mom thought that was so funny.

"I can't believe she bought that. I really can't."

Dad said it's a very practical car and Mom said she'd rather die than drive a car like that.

"Die, Roxie?"

We were sitting at dinner and me and Dad were almost done eating, but Mom had barely touched her salmon.

Olivia was in the high chair throwing applesauce.

"Yes, die." She laughed. "Mazzy, if I ever buy a Honda Civic, kill me."

I think about that as we drive down Ninth.

Mrs. Dean has no style.

My mom does.

I do not need a tighter T-shirt.

Mom would have told me if I did.

Mrs. Dean is talking about the weather and how fun summer is and what she used to do when she was a girl my age.

I am watching the houses go by and a boy is peeing in the gutter.

I look at Mrs. Dean — she's talking about junior high and her favorite class.

More houses and a girl jogging and three old ladies standing in a circle.

One of the ladies looks like she's crying.

I try to watch but it's so fast.

I take off my seatbelt and turn all the way around to watch.

"Mazzy? What are you doing?" Mrs. Dean says. "Sit down."

I turn back around and sit.

She looks over at me. "You're going to be okay. You're just going to have to grow up a little."

Blah blah.

## ME AND COLBY

Colby started acting weird at the end of the school year.

Like in PE when we had to do square dancing and the boys got to pick partners.

He didn't pick me even though I know he wanted to.

I got picked third from last and it was too bad for the boys who didn't pick me because I am very coordinated. People just don't know that.

Now Colby just wears his football pads.

And now he thinks everything is stupid.

Like snakes.

I wish we didn't have to go back to school.

I wish it could stay summer forever.

Summer with my mom not in bed.


## YOGA

First you get a mat.

Then you sit on the mat.

Then a lady comes out and says, "Let's start in Child's Pose."

Then all the people around who are mostly women but there are three men and one of the men is already sweating and one of the men has a bald head and wears a headband and the other one I can't see because he's right behind me, all of these people get on their knees and then put their heads on the floor.

Mrs. Dean is lying on the floor too.

I'm still sitting.

"Mazzy," she whispers, "just follow me." And then she puts her head on the mat between her knees.

But I don't do it. I just sit.

The lady in front says, "Set your practice. Take time to see yourself. What do you want to achieve today?"

No one answers her. No one is even looking at her except me.

She walks over. "Is this your first time?"

"No," I say.

"It's not?"

"No."

"Can I help you with anything?"

"No."

And then she leaves. Mrs. Dean looks over at me. "Mazzy, please."

She looks like she might get mad.

So I get on my knees and put my head between them. The oranges start to fall out of the bikini top so I take them out and put them by the mat. Mrs. Dean acts like she doesn't care.

I put my head back between my knees.

I kind of like sitting like that. I smash my face onto the mat — it smells like rubber bands and sweat.

The lady talks again. "Okay, concentrate on the breath. In through the nose and out through the nose."

All of a sudden there's a loud thunder of Darth Vader breaths in the room. I sit up.

No else is sitting up.

Instead they are all breathing really loud.

They are still with their faces on the mat but they are breathing really loud.

"Good. Good," the lady in charge says. "That's what we call the Ujjayi breath. Use it to set your practice. The breath will rejuvenate and restart your system."

I think about that.

Restart?

The rest of the time is like that: we have to stand up, raise our arms, bend down, jump back, do a push-up, get on our bellies, and then go into an upside down V, which the lady who is named Monica calls Downward Dog.

I have never seen a dog do this or Upward Dog, where you put your stomach on the floor and your head in the air.

The whole time we're doing all this we have to breathe like Darth Vader.

Before I do a Downward Dog, I tuck in my shirt so it won't come up.

Mrs. Dean watches me and makes a face like, "See? You should have worn a different shirt."

But I just close my eyes and restart my practice.

Most of the time I don't do what the lady says.

Some I do but I don't if I think it won't feel good like when she says, "Take the twist deeper; this is displacing stale blood and moving juices through your digestive organs."

Everyone twists and I think, stale blood?

For the next three things I just sort of do whatever I want.

Until this one: Modified Bridge Pose.

We are on our backs and she says we are going to do a Modified Bridge Pose. "This one," she says, "is excellent for relieving depression."

My heart jumps.

I look at Mrs. Dean again but she isn't looking at me. She's in a back bend.

I do the back bend and my heart won't stop.

"Lower for a breath," Monica says.

I lower.

"And now," she says, "on the inhale, pop back up."

I pop back up and start breathing like Darth Vader — even louder than Darth Vader.

I do it more than three times.

I do it like ten times while everyone else is doing a Fish Pose.

Then I do the next three things: I try to do a headstand and I can't do it but I try; I touch my toes even though my knees are bent and it hurts my back; and finally, I sit in reverse lotus and breathe.

That's when class ends — with everyone sitting cross-legged and their faces on the floor again saying something out loud that I don't understand.

When people start getting up, I keep my face on the mat and think about the Modified Bridge Pose.

Modified Bridge Pose.

"Mazzy? Are you okay?" It's Mrs. Dean talking, and I don't want to get up yet.

But I do.

"How was that?" she asks.

"Fine."

"You liked it?"

"Fine."

She gives me another one of her looks and starts to roll up her mat.

I roll up mine too and Monica the yoga lady comes over and says, "It was nice to have you in class."

"Oh."

"Did you enjoy it?"

Mrs. Dean is standing so close to me that we're touching.

"Yes," I say. "It was almost as good as the other place I usually attend."

"Oh, where is that?"

Mrs. Dean clears her throat and I don't.

Instead we all stand there and I notice that Monica has a tattoo of a star on her neck.

Finally, Mrs. Dean says, "Well, thanks for class. We better be going," and then we leave.

MODIFIED BRIDGE POSE: crayons on paper

## NORMAL

Dad made me go back to school one week after Olivia was gone.

Everything had to go back to normal. "We have to move on."

He went to work in his car and I went to school in the bus and Mom sat in the house by herself.

Part of this is Dad's fault.

## SCHOOL

Everyone at school said, Sorry. Sorry about your sister. Are you okay?
Sorry. Sorry.
My three best friends still ate lunch with me but they didn't talk like
they used to.
They just bit on their sandwiches. And bit and bit.
Before it all happened, we talked about boys and bras and how many
fries we could get on a fork.
We also talked about gymnastics because we were all going to take it
together.
After it happened, they just bit and bit and bit.
I'd rather watch *Oprah* anyway.


## OPRAH

Oprah has a personal trainer named Bob Greene.
He has natural guns like Dixie's old boyfriend Henry and he says anyone
can get in shape. Anyone.
I wonder if Norma is anyone.
I also wonder why Dixie dumped Henry and what happens when people
get dumped.

## MRS. DEAN

After yoga, Mrs. Dean takes me to the Gap.

"I don't shop here," I say.

"Of course you do." And she starts looking at something.

I sit on a place where they keep T-shirts until a lady with a nametag that says Fairy says, "You can't sit there. Sorry."

So then I sit on the ground by the jeans.

"Where's Dixie?" I ask Mrs. Dean, but she is holding up a brown blazer in the mirror so she can't answer me.

I say it louder. "I thought Dixie was going to come with us to yoga."

"Nope," she says, and holds up a gray one that looks like elephants.

"Why not? You said."

Mrs. Dean sighs and puts the blazer back. "Dixie had a little accident today so she couldn't come."

"What kind of accident?"

"It's not important."

"Why?"

"Because Dixie is always messing things up."

Mrs. Dean holds up a pink shirt now that makes her face all red.

"That makes your face all red."

Her face gets redder in the mirror.

"Thanks."

"You're welcome," I say.

"Why don't you get up and look around a bit? I'll buy you a new outfit."

"No thanks," I say.

She holds up another shirt and it is green.

It looks like baby poo. So I say, "What did Dixie do?"

She sticks her chest out and pulls the sides of the shirt around her. It doesn't look good.

"It doesn't matter what Dixie did."

Mrs. Dean looks at me and then walks to another part of the store.

I keep sitting there.

I think about Dixie.

I also think about Dixie's accident.

I wonder if it was like our accident or not that bad.

Mrs. Dean comes back with a stack of clothes and says, "Okay, let's go. Get up. We're going to the dressing room."

I sit there.

"Get up, Mazzy."

I still sit there.

"I said, get up."

The lady named Fairy is looking at us and so is a girl who looks familiar, and I wonder if she went to my school.

"Mazzy," Mrs. Dean whispers. "Now. Please get up right now. Make this a bit easier for both of us."

Then I remember. The girl's name is Holly.

I get up and say, "Hi Holly."

Holly says, "Hi Mazzy."

Mrs. Dean smiles.

So I say, "I don't usually shop here."

Mrs. Dean stops smiling and grabs my arm.

I do a karate chop in the air and then we go to the dressing room.

## OLD VAMPIRES

"Colby, what if they're old vampires?"

"How old?"

"Like grandmas."

"Are they hot?"

"Pretty hot," I say.

"How hot?"

"Hot."

"And they are vampires for sure?" he asks.

"Yeah."

"Liar."

"What?" I say.

"Your story doesn't work. When you get to be a vampire, you don't get old."

"You don't?"

"No, stupid."

"Not at all?"

"No. You become immortal. You don't age at all."

Colby gets up from the sprinkler.

"Duh," he says.

Then he says, "So no. I would not make out with an old vampire."

## DRESSING ROOM

In the dressing room I try on a jean skirt, three T-shirts, a pair of jeans, a striped thing, and four pairs of shorts.

"Well," Mrs. Dean says, "I love them all. How are we going to decide?"

I'm standing there in my underwear, which is lacy, and my bra, which has oranges in it. Mrs. Dean hasn't said anything about the oranges again.

"I like the skirt and the T-shirts," I say. And I don't really like them all that much but I guess I should get some stuff for school.

"What about this?" She holds up the pink striped thing.

"No."

"Why not? You looked so cute in it."

"No. I hate it."

And I'm being rude. Mom would say, "Mazzy, don't give her the satisfaction."

But for some reason I can't help it. Mrs. Dean is on my nerves. She's acting like she knows me.

I karate chop at her and she backs against the wall.

"What was that?" she asks, like I was really going to hit her.

"What?"

She looks at me for a while and I don't care.

Then she says, "You heard from your dad?"

I want to karate chop again so I do.

She sighs and says, "Mazzy, honey, you're acting like a little kid. You need to act your age."

I close my eyes, and we are both standing there and standing there until finally she says, "Well, I'm going to go buy these. You get dressed."

"All of them?"

"Yep. Today is your day and I thought you looked great in everything but maybe not these."

She puts a pair of shorts on the hook.

"I liked those."

She ignores me and says, "I think your Mom would agree that these are very flattering clothes."

I feel something sick in my stomach.

She's folding everything and I'm sitting on the bench still in my underwear and oranges.

"I've been wanting to do something for you and Roxie for so long and this turned out to be a fun idea."

I pick at the lace on my panties.

"Don't you think it was fun?"

Fun backwards is NUF.

"NUF," I want to say, but I don't. I don't want to act like a little kid.

She starts humming again and then says, "Okay, get dressed and I'll meet you out by the checkout," and then she's gone.

I wonder what my mom would say if she was here.

I wonder if Mom would like these clothes even a little bit.

I wonder if I look like Mom at all.

I look at myself in the mirror.

Stand up and look at everything: my face, my arms, my stomach, my legs, my butt, my everything.

This is everything.

And I don't look like her.

I take the oranges out and jump on them so that juice gets all over the floor.

I smash them and wipe them all over the walls and then someone says, "Hey, what's going on in there?"

Some shoes are outside the door — right next to the door — almost in the stall.

I freeze.

A knock on the door.

"Is everything okay?"

"Yep," I say.

The shoes are still there.

And then they leave.

I push all the orange leftovers into a pile in the corner of the dressing room and put the shorts we aren't buying on top of them.

Then I get dressed and leave.


## BACK BENDS

When I get home from yoga with bags from the Gap, I go straight to her room.

She is in her yellow nightgown and she is looking at the ceiling.

"Mom," I whisper.

She keeps looking up, and I sit in the chair by the bed.

"Mom," I say louder. She turns her head a little toward me but is still looking at the ceiling.

Then I say, "I went to yoga. Mrs. Dean took me."

She blinks.

"I think you might've liked it or maybe not."

Blinks again.

"Is yoga stupid?"

Blink.

"She got me these clothes."

I pull out the skirt and the T-shirts and the pink thing.

She closes her eyes and breathes really deep. I hold the clothes up for when she opens her eyes.

She doesn't.

She just breathes deep.

So I say, "Actually, your breathing is very good. It's a rejuvenating breath called Ujjiya or something and that's another thing I wanted to show you."

I put the clothes down and I pull the covers off her.

But first I open the window and the blinds so she can reset her system.

Then I say, "Keep breathing really deep through your nose."

She does.

Then I say, "Okay, I'm going to help you do something from yoga. It will help you, I think."

Her eyes are still closed but she is doing the breath and it is almost like Darth Vader.

So then I try to do this but it isn't easy.

I say, "It's called Modified Bridge Pose." I put my hand on her shoulders and say, "Bend your knees."

She doesn't so I have to make her bend her knees. Her nightgown falls down to her stomach.

I look at her thighs.

Blue.

Blue white and red.

Like the flag.

She doesn't move or try to cover up. She just keeps breathing.

"Good, Mom," I said. "Good concentration." Then I said, "Now get on your shoulders."

But I can't really explain what I mean because it's not easy to explain. I say, "Like put your arms underneath your body and curve onto your shoulders."

She doesn't and I am holding her knees so they will stay bent.

I let them go to show her the shoulder part, and they go back down.

"Mom, you have to do some of it," I say. Her eyes are still closed.

So I get her knees back up and I try again. I say, "Go up with your butt and stomach in the air but your shoulders on the ground."

She lies there. Breathing.

"Mom, please try this. Please."

She doesn't move.

"Please?"

I let go of her knees again and they slide back down.

I can do this.

So I lie down on the bed.

"Like this, Mom." I do one. "Just do what I'm doing. It's called Modified Bridge Pose. It's supposed to help."

She won't open her eyes.

"Open your eyes, Mom."

Please open your eyes and try this. Something is starting to come up my throat but I bite on it.

Mom's eyes are still closed. She is breathing deep and my tongue is bleeding.

Finally I say, "Mom, do you think I act like a little kid?"
Nothing.

Later, when Bill comes over to help Mom, he yells to the front room, "What are all these clothes doing on the bed?"
I switch the channel to *Wheel of Fortune*.
"It's one thing to have all your crap on the floor, but you can't have stuff on the bed. Okay? You've got to keep stuff off the bed, Mazzy."
Bill would be bad at *Wheel of Fortune*.


## NONI JUICE

One time I gave Mom a cup of noni juice.
Norma gave it to me because she found it in her fridge and said, "Maybe your mom would like this. It's supposed to be healthy."
"What is it?"
"Exotic fruit juice delivers superior antioxidants."
She was reading from the label.
"What are antioxidants?" I asked.
She shrugged. "Not sure, but I've heard this juice fixes everything."
"Everything?"
"That's what I heard, on the Web site and around," she said.
"Why do you have it?"
"Even if I don't look like it, I'm trying to be healthy."
"Oh," I said, and pulled another weed because I help her pull weeds almost every day now.
I got up and sat with her at the table.

Instead of lemonade, we had Fresca and a bottle of noni juice.

"Does it work?" I asked. I don't like Norma's lawn chair because my butt was going through the plastic slats.

"Umm, I don't know."

"You haven't tried it?"

"Not yet. I don't like how it smells. Plus I just buy the stuff; I don't drink it."

I opened the lid and smelled it: barf.

Then we ate Twinkies and I ate three almonds from a bowl she brought out.

"Can I take this home?"

"Of course you can," she said, and handed me another Twinkie.

Twinkies at sunset: oils on canvas

## OLIVIA'S ALBUM

So that night after two reruns, I put the juice in one of her yellow cups and take it with the sorbet and pills.

I almost drop the tray when I get in there because she is sitting in the chair by the dresser looking at the album.

"You're up."

She turns a page and doesn't look at me.

It is Olivia's album. The one she keeps under the bed. She'd gotten up and crawled under the bed.

I hold my breath and she turns another page.

Then I say again, "You're up." Another page.

Her hair is matted against her head and she'd put on an Eeyore sweatshirt that I'd gotten from Disneyland when I went with Dad on a special broadcast.

She didn't like that sweatshirt.

"Mom?"

Still nothing, just another page.

I step over a pile of pants and then some shoes and put the tray on her bed table.

"Mom?"

Nothing.

I sit on the bed and watch her. Her face is so hard. So white and hard and skinny.

I look at my hands and sit. And sit. I sit like that and she sits like that for over an hour. She starts the album over and over and I sit and sit.

"Mom? Do you want your pills?"

The sorbet is a puddle and I don't know if the noni juice has to be cold.

"Mom?"

A while later I am lying on the bed.

On my side watching her.

Then on my back.

On my side again.

On my back.

Page after page after page.

I wake up the next morning and she is next to me — her knees in her chest and her breathing heavy.

The sorbet puddle is still there but the pills and noni are gone.

And one more thing; her hand is touching my hair.

## DAD

One week after the text message, Dad calls again.

"I'm going to try to come home this weekend."

I'm melting eleven marshmallows because Lisa dropped some off.

"Did you hear me, Maz?"

The microwave beeps.

"Am I on speakerphone?"

I open it and the marshmallows aren't done.

"Maz."

I push .30 and start.

"Maz . . . Maz, answer me."

I turn on the light and watch the marshmallows go around and around.

"Mazzy, pick up the phone and talk to me right now."

The microwave beeps again but they still aren't done. I check with a chopstick.

"Mazeline, if you don't pick up the phone right now . . ."

I pick up the phone and say: "What?"

"I'm going to try to come home this weekend so we can sort things out."

I don't say anything.

"I have had several long discussions with Mrs. Peet."

I bite my lip. I don't know how to feel because I don't want him to put her in a place.

Everything is fine.

We're fine.

I want to tell him that.

But then I also want to tell him he can come home. He should come home. We need him.

"Okay," I finally say, and I take the marshmallows out anyway.

He's quiet for awhile and I stir the marshmallows.

"Is everything okay?"

"Yes."

"What are you doing?"

"Making Peking duck for me and Mom."

"Peking duck this time, huh?"

He sort of laughs.

He says: "Getting a little fancy these days, eh?"

"I'm serious, Dad. Mom said she wanted Peking duck so I'm making it."

He's quiet.

I eat some marshmallow but it's too hot and I burn my tongue. I drop the phone and it hangs up.

## DAD

Dad and Mom used to dance.

Late at night when we were supposed to be asleep.

Mom would throw back her head and laugh and Dad would pick her up.

"Stop it, Dave," she'd say.

"What?" And he twirled her around and around.

"You're going to hurt your back."

"Well, I guess I should stop, then," he'd say, and keep twirling and twirling and twirling.

I used to lay on the floor and watch them from the hallway.

Watch them laugh.

I'd lay there until maybe Dad saw me and he'd say, "Well, looks like someone is in big old trouble," and I'd scream "No!" and he'd put Mom on the couch, and her face. I can see her face.

All giggly.

I'd start down the hall but he'd catch me. He always caught me and then it was me laughing and twirling and everything was how it was supposed to be.

My mom used to love my dad and my dad used to love my mom.

And they both used to love me.

He went for a one-week audition for ESPN 360. One week became forever.


## NEW FOOD

Lisa comes by and she has four big bags of groceries.

"My dad's coming home for the weekend," I say.

"I know," she says. And she starts emptying milk and bread and everything we haven't had for a long long time.

"He called you?"

She doesn't answer but instead pulls out a box of cookies.

"Why so much stuff?"

Another box of cookies and a roasted chicken.

She still doesn't answer and she's slamming things down on the counter.

When she finally has everything out, I say, "Aren't some things for you and José and the kids?"

"No," she says, and looks at me with bad eyes. "I never take things home for José and the kids."

"Okay," I say, and I get it.

And she's still looking at me, her round chin shaking like she might cry or murder.

"Okay," I say.

"I'll be back next week," she says, and she leaves.

Lisa is usually nice to me.

I wonder what Dad said. I wonder how Dad thinks he can fix things. He just messes things up even though we do have Soft Batch cookies now.

## KIWIS

Lisa didn't buy any oranges.

But she did buy kiwis.

Five kiwis.

But a kiwi is the wrong size. In the mirror it looks pokey. Or too round. I even try it with a shirt over it but the fuzz makes me itch.

She also bought a cantaloupe.
I don't try it.

## OLIVIA

I try not to think about her.
It's easier.

I might mow the lawn for when Dad gets here. I also should clean up the art room.
But I don't think I will.

## COLBY

Colby says, "You went to yoga?"

"Uh-huh."

He's on his bike and he's weaving between things like a broom, a football helmet, and three Tootsie Rolls.

I'm sitting in the sprinklers.

"Yoga is stupid."

"Kind of."

"My mom is stupid."

"Oh," I say.

"It's dumb she made you go."

"It's okay," I say.

He keeps riding. And then he says, "Me and my dad told her you were okay but sometimes she just does whatever."

"Oh," I say.

I'm about to ask him about Dixie but then he crashes.

And he says, "Oooooooooooo," and he is bleeding.

I get up to help him but he runs inside.

I try his bike and I don't crash.

COLBY'S BIKE WRECK: pastels on cardboard

## MISSING NORMA

Norma and I had thought of a few plans to help Mom.

The noni juice.

Ocean music.

Hypnosis.

Oprah's feel-good tips.

We thought of a lot of things.

I even thought maybe Norma could stay with us and we could tell Mrs.
Peet that she was my aunt and she was going to take care of us.

"Would you do that, Norma?"

"Sure, honey. I'd love to." She took a bite of a Twinkie. "But I don't
know that your dad would like it."

"Oh," I said. She was right. Norma had offered to stay with us when it
happened last August but Dad said no. He said we were fine. We're fine.

We're a family and we'll survive this.

Now he's gone. And Mom's in bed.

Fine.

## MOUNT RUSHMORE

In South Dakota there are four presidents carved into a mountain.

On the Discovery channel, they said it took fourteen years to make their faces and they almost added a lady — Susan B. Anthony — but then they didn't.

I tell Colby and he says, "So?"

I say, "Do you think that's weird?"

He says, "Not really."

I say, "Have you ever seen it before?"

He says, "What?"

I say, "Mount Rushmore."

He says, "Uh, yeah. I go there every freaking week because it's so interesting. Who doesn't want to look at presidents' faces carved into a mountain?"

Then he pulls a green thing from his teeth and says, "Do you want to see the engine of the Dean Machine?"

"Okay," I say. So we do.

While we are looking, a couple of guys I don't know ride by on their bikes. Colby sort of sits up and starts to wave when one of them yells, "Hey Colby, you suck."

Colby turns red.

"You're not going to make the team, reject." Their laughs trail behind them.

Immediately, Oprah's advice pops into my head and I yell, "Stop that. I don't like it!"

They don't hear.

I look at Colby. He looks even more red. "You don't suck," I say.

His lip is trembling so I say, "What's that?" And I point to this black greasy thing.

It's the radiator.

After we look at the engine, Colby gets us some otter pops just like we used to eat.

Mount Rushmore but with me and Colby instead of two of the guys: pastels on canvas

## OLIVIA

Olivia got a gobstopper stuck in her nose once.

They were my gobstoppers and Mom said I should have been watching more closely.

Olivia just laughed and I smiled and Mom was trying not to because I was in trouble.

## NORMA

The day before Dad is supposed to get here everything is still.

The air is hot and heavy and no one is outside.

Not Colby because the Dean Machine is gone.

And not even Norma even though we usually pull weeds at this time.

I think about going over there but instead I turn on the sprinklers and walk through them four times and then turn them off.

Then I go inside and get the Q-tips.

I come back outside and sit on the curb and I see Mr. Grobin under his car with his legs sticking out.

It's so hot.

I wonder if he knows where Norma is.

I almost yell: Where's Norma?

But instead I get a Q-tip and I start digging in my ear and watching Mr. Grobin.

I like to dig in my ear even though in fifth grade Mr. Porter said you shouldn't dig. You should just let the wax come out on its own.

But I like to wait and wait and wait and then finally get the Q-tips and you can get big balls of wax smeared on the ends.

I like to see how much I can get and I look at it.

I like to look and see how much there is and if it's more than last time.

I'm doing that when Mr. Grobin comes out from under his car.

He doesn't say anything to me even though he looks at me.

I wave.

He walks over to Norma's house and goes inside.

Then I dig again in the same ear.

Not a lot.

I put the used Q-tips on the sidewalk and lie down to rest before I do the other ear — I don't want to do it all so fast.

That's when the ambulance comes.


## AMBULANCE

The ambulance comes swerving into our neighborhood and stops in front of Norma's house.

I almost yell: "You have the wrong house."

Because Norma is fine. I pulled weeds with her yesterday.

I almost yell: "She's fine."

But instead I sit and watch because I haven't seen an ambulance that close since it happened with us and I can't move.

They just pull up to her house and then people start coming out from all over the neighborhood.

Just like with us.

"What's going on?" someone yells.

Just like with us.

Where's Mr. Grobin?

I'm just sitting with my Q-tips and staring.

I am about to yell: "Nothing's wrong with Norma," but I don't.

The men go inside and I sit.

The men come outside and Norma is on a stretcher with a thing on her face. Mr. Grobin is walking next to them.

That's when I stand up. There's something wrong.

I can't breathe.

Not Norma.

Not Norma.

Mr. Grobin is talking to one of the men.

I just stand.

I stand while they put Norma in the back.

I stand while they close the doors.

I stand while Mr. Grobin runs back toward his house.

I stand while the other people who are standing around start going home.

I stand until they start pulling out into the middle of the road with the siren screaming, and then I run.

The tears are coming hard down my face. I run out in the middle of the road in front of the ambulance.

THE AMBULANCE: pencil on paper

## NORMA'S AMBULANCE

When the ambulance screeches and doesn't hit me, the driver is yelling, and Mr. Grobin, who had run to his house, is running back to Norma's when everything happens.

"Mazzy!" Mr. Grobin yells.

But I am hysterical because Norma is in the ambulance dying.

The driver gets out and says, "What are you doing?"

"What's wrong with her?" I yell. "Is she dead?"

"No," says the driver.

"No," says Mr. Grobin.

"No," says everyone.

I am shaking and Mr. Grobin is pulling me away from the ambulance toward the side of the road.

"Sorry about this, sorry. She's a good friend of the lady in there. Sorry, go ahead and take her. We'll be right behind."

I am still shaking and the driver runs back to the ambulance.

Mr. Grobin sits me on the curb and waves the ambulance on as it goes around the corner.

A few lingering neighbors are looking at us and Mr. Grobin tells them, "Get the hell out of here."

Then he sits by me. I scooch away. Tears are running down my face and I do not cry.

"She's going to be okay," he says. I scooch farther away. "I promise you."

I wipe my face and snot on my T-shirt.

Mr. Grobin gives me a rag that has grease on it from his pocket. I wipe more snot and then give it back.

"How do you know she's going to be okay?"

"Because this happens every once in a while. Norma's been under a lot of stress. You probably know that Norma is diabetic."

I didn't know.

"She just had an insulin reaction. Have you heard of that?"

"Yes," I say. It was on *Oprah*.

"This is not out of the ordinary; it's just usually Norma can fix it before it gets this bad."

I don't know what he's talking about but I'm glad he is talking. When it happened with us, no one talked to me.

"What's an insulin reaction?"

He tells me.

"But she eats Twinkies."

"She eats a lot of things she shouldn't. She's trying to be better about it but she doesn't have a whole lot of self-control."

I cough.

He looks at me and then says, "Do you want to come with me to the hospital?"

"No," I say.

He puts his hand on my back and says, "She's going to be okay."

"Okay," I say. And then he leaves.

I sit there for a long time afterward.

Norma is sick.

She probably can't take care of us.

And she could die.

I don't do the other ear.

Instead I just go home and lie on my bed.

I see a spider crawling up the door.

Then it's behind the blinds.

I wonder how many spiders are in our house.

## MOM'S SPYDER

After the Range Rover was gone, Dad bought Mom a black convertible Spyder.

"It's an awesome car, Roxie," he said.

This was when Mom had stopped eating and was beginning to become how she is now.

She didn't answer him.

"Don't you want to take a ride in it?"

"No."

"It's a convertible. You've always wanted a convertible."

"No."

"Well, Mazzy and I are going for a ride to get ice cream whether you come or not, huh, Mazzy?"

I looked at Mom. She was sitting in her nightgown at the kitchen table. It was eleven in the morning on a Saturday and I'd never seen her in her nightgown except in her room and I'd never seen her just sit. Especially on Saturdays.

"Mom," I said. "Just come."

"No."

She was holding a cup of milk and Dad and I were both watching her.

"Just for a little ride."

"No."

We sat like that for awhile until Dad finally said, "Okay, let's go, Mazzy."

"Mom?" I whispered.

She was staring.

We got in the Spyder and Dad swore.

I didn't say anything.
We went for a ride but we didn't get ice cream.

Mom has never ridden in the Spyder.
Not once.

## COLBY

Colby knocks on the window.
I am putting a hard-boiled egg on my sandwich.
And then I'm trying to balance a chocolate chip Soft Batch on top of it.
It keeps falling off.
That's when he knocks and whisper-yells, "Mazzy."
This is the first time this summer he has come to talk to me without me yelling first. I want to hurry and see what he wants but I have to get the Soft Batch to stay.
"Mazzy," he says again.
"Hang on," I say.
"What are you doing?"
I don't answer because I almost have it.
But it keeps falling off so I just go to the window. "What?" I say.
"Can I come in?"
His face is pressed against the glass and his glasses are off.
"What?" I say.
"Can I come in?" he says louder.
"What?"

"Can I come in? What's your problem?"

I look around. I've been trying to clean for Dad so there are rags and buckets and Windex and newspaper and stuff all over.

Plus Soft Batch cookies spread on the table.

"Okay," I say.

Then his face is still pressed against the glass.

"I said okay," I say.

Still pressed. He isn't moving.

"What are you doing?"

"Trying to figure out how to get in."

Then I remember I had put signs on the two doors: "Do not disturb. No one can enter these doors. Maintenance."

I'd put them up in case Mrs. Peet came over.

I say to him, "You mean the signs?"

"Yeah."

I bite my lip.

"Yeah, you probably can't come in," I say.

"I can't?"

"I guess not. I forgot about the doors. If I let you in then I have to let everyone in."

I feel bad he can't come in because this is the first time since Mom got sick that he wants to, but I didn't know if Mrs. Peet was watching our house or something.

Then he says, "What about through the window?"

I think about it and then I say, "Hang on."

I put my hair behind my ears, get up, do a karate chop, and then go to check on Mom even though Colby's face is pressed on my kitchen window. I've never let a boy through the window before.

## MOM

Her door is closed.

I never leave the door closed.

I look down the hall. No one.

"Is someone here? Bill?"

No one answers except my mom's voice from in her room. "You can come in, Mazzy."

It's loud and really her voice.

I look at the door.

It's brown.

Then I open it and she is sitting up and sort of normal-looking.

"Mom?"

"Hi, baby," she says.

"You're awake."

"Uh-huh." There is color in her face.

"What are you doing?"

"Just thinking."

"Are you feeling better?"

"A little bit."

A little bit. A little bit. She is feeling a little bit better and she is talking to me.

"Dad's coming home tomorrow," I say.

"I know." She smiles. "You've been missing him, huh?"

I'm confused. "You know he's coming home?"

"Yep."

"How do you know?"

"You've been telling me every day for a week, baby."

I'm still standing in the doorway when she says that and I slump.

"You mean you heard all that?"

"I guess. I mean, yeah. But it was sort of like a dream."

I bite my lip and watch her move toward the edge of the bed. "Are you getting up?"

"I think so. I think I might take a shower."

"Really?"

She looks at me and smiles. It's the first time I've seen her smile in a month.

"You don't think I need to? Do I smell that good?" she says.

I knock my head on the door frame. "It's just, you don't, it's just —"

"I know," she says. "It's okay."

"Mom, I'm sorry about your room."

For the first time she sort of looks around. "What about it?"

"I'm sorry about my clothes and the books and the shoes and everything."

She smiles again and says, "Go let your friend in."

She'd heard? She'd been listening. She'd heard.

"Are you sure you're okay? You don't need help?"

"I'm okay," she says.

I turn and start down the hall, but then she says, "Maz?"

"Yeah, Mom?"

"Could you shut the door?"

She is still sitting on the edge of her bed like it's a regular Thursday.

"Okay."

I shut the door and stand there for awhile.

I stand there.

And stand there.

And stand there.

I stand there until I hear Colby knocking on the window again.

My mom is taking a shower and Colby Dean is waiting for me to let him in.

## COLBY IN THE WINDOW

"So?" he says.

"So what?" I say back, and I put a strand of hair in my mouth. I wish I still had the oranges.

"How do I get in?"

"How come you want to? It's eight o'clock."

"Just do," he says.

I think about that as I lean against the counter.

"Okay."

Then I open the window and pull off the screen and Colby climbs into my house.

## OLIVIA

Olivia is or I guess was nine years younger than me.

She never saw a boy come through our window.

## SUGAR

Colby crawls through the window and knocks down the calendar from last year that's still up, breaks two glasses, and gets his hands all wet because the counter has juice on it.

"Sick," he says.

"Sorry," I say.

"Don't you clean?"

I look around the kitchen.

It never really looks all that good since I got in charge.

I don't say anything.

He washes his hands and then sits at the table so I sit at the table.

"Do you want a marshmallow?"

"Okay."

I get out the bag.

"Do you want them cooked?"

"No," he says, and stuffs three in his mouth.

Then we are quiet. Colby's eyes are a little cross-eyed without his glasses and he has spiked his hair down the middle. He looks sort of weird. Not like Colby.

"Did you do your hair?"

"Uh no, Bill Clinton did it for me," he says, even though his mouth is full of white foam.

"Oh," I say. "I like it."

"Of course you do," he says, and he looks down at his arms. "Do you think I'm getting natural guns?"

"Not really."

"You don't?"

"No. I mean, not really."

"Oh."

"Why? Do you want them?"

"Sort of."

And then we sit.

Then he says, "I'm probably getting contacts."

"Oh," I say.

Then he says, "Colored ones."

"Oh."

"Do you want to know which color?"

"Okay."

"Yellow."

I eat a marshmallow and he's just looking at me.

"Don't you think that'd be cool?"

I eat another one.

Then I say, "How's Dixie?"

Colby turns sort of red. "She's cool." He stuffs three more marshmallows in his mouth.

Then he says, "My mom said she's trashy."

"Trashy? She said that about her sister?"

Colby nods. "She just said that she dresses slutty and that she better do it while she can because Mom says her boobs are going to drop and her butt will get big."

"Oh," I say.

I eat another marshmallow and my stomach is getting inflated.

Colby is drawing circles on the wood table with his finger. "I know it's weird how my mom says stuff like that about her own sister."

"Oh," I say.

He looks at me. "Aunt Dixie did say one thing about you, though."

"She did?"

"Well, about your . . ." and then he mouths the word MOM and looks out the door toward the hall.

"What?" I say, but I say it soft.

"They were over for a barbecue and me and Aunt Dixie got left alone at the table."

He takes another marshmallow and says, "Can you melt this one for me?"

"Later," I say. I want to know what Dixie said.

"Okay," he says. Then he wipes something from his nose and looks at it.

"What did she say?" He is taking forever.

"She started asking things about you and your mom and crap."

"Like what?"

"Like," he says, and then he stops and his eyes drop.

"What?"

"Like she'd heard what had happened to Olivia and all that." He stops again and we sit. Then he says, "And she said it was so crappy how people talk about your mom the way they do."

I feel something sink in my stomach.

He looks at me.

I look back and say, "What are people saying?"

"I don't know. I didn't even know she'd know people who even knew your mom but I guess my mom and dad say stuff." He pauses, pulls a marshmallow apart, and then sticks it to his arm. "Plus, everyone knows because of your dad and everything."

Dad.

He sticks another one on his arm and doesn't look at me.

I get up and put the marshmallows on a plate.

"Do you like them burned or not burned?"

"Whatever," he says. He is making a tower now.

I press start on the microwave and am watching it go around and around when he says, "Randy asks about it too. Almost everyone does."

The microwave beeps but I don't move.

"I just say I don't know."

He turns in his chair. "Is that what I should say?"

I shrug.

He looks at his shoes again and then says, "Do you guys have any sugar? I was supposed to come over and ask for sugar."

COLBY AND ME WITH MARSHMALLOWS: crayon on paper

## DAD AND ESPN 360

It all started when Dad got a phone call from the network.

He was up for the job.

Mom didn't want him to take it.

"Roxie, this is huge. This is what we've been waiting for."

"I thought we were waiting for ABC," she said.

They were talking in the kitchen and me and Olivia were watching *Barney* or something in the living room.

They never fought.

Except about jobs.

Dad didn't say anything.

Mom did. "Dave, this is ESPN 360. This is curling and foosball," she said.

"Give me a break," he said, and he was louder than normal.

All I could think was, Please don't let us move. Please don't let us move.

Things were good — and before we got here we had to move and move and move. I liked it here.

Mom didn't want to leave because she had lots of friends and she had her art studio and her business and Dad was making money as the local sports anchor and people liked him and everything was how it was supposed to be.

They kept talking and talking and finally Dad yelled something. It made Olivia jump, and she looked over at me, her fat cheeks red and her mouth open.

"It's okay," I said. But then Dad yelled again and Olivia's face started to scrunch up and soon she was crying.

Mom ran into the room yelling, "See what you did, Dave. You've upset Olivia."

Dad followed her and watched her pick Olivia up. She was whimpering and put her head on Mom's shoulder.

I looked at the carpet.

"This is a family decision, Dave. What's best for the family."

Dad stood in the doorway, silent, while Mom rocked Olivia back and forth. The air was heavy, and this moment I remembered so well.

It's almost like it's frozen.

He said, "Things are going to change, Roxie. What works for you doesn't always work for me. Things change."

And then he walked over, kissed Olivia on the nose, nodded at me, and went out the front door.

Three days later it happened.


## ART

I never tried to do art before.

She always asked if I wanted her to teach me but I didn't.

I don't know why.

Now I want her to.


In Mom's art room I've made it better even if it's messier.

Like I pulled out her paintings and put them on the walls.

She used to have them out plus some of her drawings of us and the finger painting Olivia had done, but after everything happened, she took them all down.

Instead, she put up prints of van Gogh or Klimt or someone famous.

Not her own stuff and not our stuff.

Right after she did it I asked her, "Where are all our paintings?" She was scribbling something on a pad of paper at her worktable and didn't respond.

"Mom?"

Still scribbling.

"Mom?"

She jumped. "Oh, Mazzy. What do you need?" She sounded mad.

"Nothing," I said, and then I left and watched TV.

The room looks better now with her stuff and my stuff and Olivia's finger painting.

## BOOBS

I made a chart about boobs.

There are many different kinds.

Norma's are droopy like melons.

Mrs. Peet's are big but pushed together and it's because of a bra.

Dixie's are round and straight out.

Mom's are little hills.

Mine are bumps.

BOOB CHART: pen on paper

## DIXIE

I think Dixie understands me.
I like her bikini and how she doesn't care.
Plus, Mrs. Dean doesn't like her so I do.


## ART CLASS

Mom told all her students that she wasn't teaching for a while.
"How long?"
"I don't know."
"Well, should I plan on bringing him next month?"
"No."
"I'm so sorry to bug you, but he loves these classes and we paid for three months in advance."
No response from Mom.
"Are you okay?"
No response from Mom.
Mom was just standing at the front door and I was standing behind her, and Mrs. Willis, whose kid Seth had been taking lessons for six months, was talking through the screen door. Mom wouldn't let anyone in.
"Umm, well. So I guess we'll just wait."
"Do that," Mom said.
"You have no idea?"
Mom was in her bathrobe and she was slumped.
I wanted to tell Mrs. Willis to shut up and leave.
But she still talked and Mom still slumped. "Is there anything I can do?"

"No."

Mrs. Willis looked past her at me — she sort of gave me a look like please help but I made my face stone like Mom's.

"Some of the other moms have been wondering too."

Stone.

Mom walked away and I was left there standing with Mrs. Willis.

"Go away," I said, and I shut the door.

Now, since the art room is mine for a while, I act like Mom and lock the door.

And I turn on her CDs.

With her music and her paintings and the smell of oil, I can almost imagine everything back how it was.


MOM'S STUDIO: watercolor on wall

## COLBY AND THE SPYDER

I give Colby the sugar but then he doesn't leave.
Instead we go outside and sit in the Spyder.
We only do it because Colby begs me.
I don't like the Spyder so much.

Colby wants to be behind the wheel. "This is such a cool car."

We came out the back door because Colby says the signs say no entrance, not no exit, which is true.

So we're sitting there and he says, "Did your dad ever let you drive it?"

"Me? No."

"Steer?"

"No."

No one has really driven it since Dad bought it. It just sits.

"I've driven the Dean Machine."

"You have?"

"Yeah. Tons of times."

"Oh," I say.

"And I could drive this thing too. I could smoke some pavement with this."

I look at the rearview mirror while he's talking. It's black outside. And stars with just a sliver moon.

"How fast do you think this could go?" he asks, and he is massaging the steering wheel.

"I don't know." I wonder if Mom is in the shower.

"Fast," he says.

Then we sit and Colby has his hands on the wheel and I have my hands in my lap.

Colby starts making vrooming noises like we're driving.

I just sit.

Mom is inside taking a shower.

She's back. Things are going to be back to normal, even with Colby.

A light goes on at Colby's.

"I gotta go," he says.

"Yeah," I say.

Then he says, "Thanks for saying I don't suck."

I smile.

And then he says, "I think McKinley Prep is going to be stupid."

"Me too," I say.

And then he does something weird.

He puts his hand on my head — like he's my grandma or something.

I don't know why but my stomach flips.

I look at him and he is looking at me. Weird-like.

"What?" I say.

He turns red again and says, "Nothing." And then he gets out and runs home.

## SOMEONE ELSE

After Colby leaves, I stay in the Spyder.

In the dark, I feel like someone else.

Dad is coming home.

Mom is in the shower.

Colby put his hand on my head.

## NORMA

I am about to get out when I see a car pull into Norma's.

It's Norma's red car.

I sink down in my seat.

Mr. Grobin goes around and helps Norma out of the car.

She's wearing her yellow T-shirt and tie-dye stretch pants and she's walking really slowly.

Part of me wants to run over there or yell or do something.

Instead I sit scrunched up in the Spyder.

She's sick and she didn't tell me.

She almost died.

I scrunch up even more.


## MOM

Inside I put the marshmallow bag in the trash and try to wipe up the counter.

The shower isn't on.

"Mom," I yell.

Wait.

"Mom?"

Wait.

"Mom, do you want your pills?"

Maybe she is in the shower drying off.

I get the sorbet and the pills and a cup of noni, which maybe is the reason she is feeling so good, and go to her room.

She isn't there.

"Mom?" No answer but the light in her bathroom is on.

"Mom?" I knock on the door.

Nothing. I try the knob. It's locked. "Mom?"

Knock again. "Mom?"

I put my ear to the door — I can hear something but I can't tell what it is. Like a buzzing sound.

"Mom? What are you doing?"

She doesn't answer.

"Mom, open the door."

No answer.

"Please, Mom. Open the door."

Nothing.

Please no please no please no.

I pound on the door. "Mom! Open the door!" Pound and pound and pound on the door.

"Mom, please. Please open the door." I pound and pound and pound until my fist is red and my throat hurts from yelling.

I slide to the ground and accidentally knock the sorbet and pills and noni over. The black noni spirals on the white carpet and the sorbet falls in a big green pile.

I am breathing deep and watching the noni slowly spread and touch the sorbet. Then the two are together — pushing against each other.

I'm thinking they would mix but instead they push at each other and make spikes — like they're fighting for space.

I put my finger where they touch and trace them together into a spiral — a noni and sorbet spiral around and around and around and around.

## FUNERAL

At the funeral, Dad spoke.

He wore his pink shirt and the tie he wore when he was recognized by his network — his lucky tie that cost over 200 dollars.

He got a haircut and new shoes and he looked like he was supposed to.

He tried to have Mom do her hair. "You'll feel better."

But Mom just sat in front of the mirror and wouldn't move.

Dad's eyes were tired.

"Roxie, please. We have to leave in fifteen minutes."

I was sitting on the toilet, watching her get ready.

Since it happened, I didn't like to be alone. I followed Mom wherever she went. I slept on the floor in her room. I ate when she ate. I did what she did.

She never said I couldn't. She never said she was mad.

So I sat on the toilet, my hair a mess too.

"Mazzy, get up and get going," Dad said. His body almost took up the entire doorway. I never realized how big he was.

I looked at Mom. She didn't move, just sat looking blankly at the mirror.

The day before, Dad had gone out and got us both new clothes. He got Mom a silk gray shirt and a black skirt that was a little too big even though he took one of her other skirts to size it.

It had been a week and Mom had already lost weight.

He got me a purple dress.

"Purple?" I said when he got back. He shrugged. "The lady said it'd be good for this kind of thing."

The dress was bulky — too big everywhere. So Mom and me, we looked like sacks. Dad looked like a TV sports anchor with a shirt my mom had picked out.

After I put on the dress, I was going to go to the kitchen to get some water but then I saw Dad with his head in his hands.

He was shaking.

I wasn't thirsty anymore.


We sat in the front pew.

Dad sat at the stand because he was talking.

The casket was right there. Right in front of me and Mom. It looked like a doll box. Like one of Olivia's doll beds.

Pink.

Silver.

Shining.

The picture of Olivia at Newport beach sitting on top — the one we took the year before on our family vacation.

Next to Mom was Agnes and her five kids and then Ted her husband. They were the only family we had and they flew all the way from Kansas, which cost them over a thousand dollars. They had to get a hotel too because there obviously wasn't room at our house and that was fine and everything, but Ted had a new job and it was not easy to get work off and to lose all that money.

"Oh," said Mom.

I think Norma was there too.

The Deans.

I don't remember if Mr. Grobin was there but I don't think he was.

My old best friends.

And then a whole bunch of people from the church and from Mom's art classes.

Dad's people were there too. His boss named Jerry who told me once that my face was a pumpkin, some other sports guys and three football players who played for the Skins. Dad was excited about that. "They didn't need to come all that way."

The whole church was full.

Dad had his TV voice when he gave his talk.

At the end he said this: "I love my wife. I love my daughters." It was the first time his voice broke. He cleared his throat. "This is what God intended. It was Olivia's time. Even though we weren't ready for it, my family will get through this."

Everyone nodded. Cried. Whispered.

I just sat and so did Mom.

Afterward, we stood and shook people's hands.

I didn't know that was how funerals worked.


Box Olivia was in: pencil on paper

## SMASHED

Afterward at our house, people were everywhere.

Dad had hired a cleaning lady and got a caterer and we had too much food because people brought stuff anyway.

In the family room, I was sitting in the corner on the couch.

There were voices and ladies in black and fat men and people laughing and some kids running around. I sat and watched the shoes.

Then one pair of brown shoes with a buckle said, "Why not an open casket?"

The other pair, high heels, black, said, "Are you kidding? She was all smashed up. It was horrific."

The other: "Really? It was that bad?"

Black shoes: "Umm, yeah. Believe me, there was no possibility of an open casket."

Smashed up.

I closed my eyes.

## MOM?

I put my hand on the door.

"Mom? Please open the door."

I hear a muffled sound. Her voice.

Then I remember the screwdriver.

Once when Mom was in a lesson, Olivia had locked herself in the bathroom.

She wouldn't open the door and Dad was at work and I couldn't get Olivia out.

I didn't want to tell Mom so I tried everything. A credit card like on TV, a butter knife, a hammer, a piece of paper.

Nothing worked and Olivia was crying. Finally, I got a screwdriver and put it in the lock and it twisted for about three minutes. Something clicked.

I pushed open the door and there was Olivia — tear-streaked face and her dark curls plastered to her head.

I never told Mom about that. I didn't want her to know because I was really watching TV when I was supposed to be watching Olivia.

I was always in charge of her and I was always messing up.

But at least this mess-up lets me get in to Mom.


## MIRACLES

When Mom was pregnant, she always peed.

One time at dinner, Mom had to go to the bathroom three times.

At the movies, four times.

Dad called her Miss Piss.

"Oh, there's my Miss Piss."

Mom would throw a pillow at him and I'd write Miss Piss in my notebook.

My teacher said, "What's Miss Piss?"

"My mom. She pees all the time."

Teacher looked at me funny. "Did you just say what I think you said?"

But I'd be coloring or doing my handwriting and not caring what she said.

We were all very happy because they had to do operations to get Mom pregnant, but it worked. Olivia was a miracle.

"You were a miracle too," Dad said.

"I was?"

"Yeah," he said. "You and Olivia are both our miracles."

"Good," I said.

At home Mom would be laughing and singing and Dad would come home early.

Mom was going to make the art room the nursery, but I said, "She should sleep in my room."

"Baby, you don't want a newborn in with you."

"Yes, I do."

And I did.

So my room was the nursery, and me and Mom found all sorts of cool things to paint and do to my room.

## SONG

There's this one song: *If a thing is hard to do, I'll not sit and cry. I'll just sing a merry song and try try try.*

*Tra la la la la la la la Tra la la la la la Tra la la la la la la la Try Try Try.*

I make that song go in my head to stop everything. To make everything stop.

It's a stupid song I learned in choir.

## OKAY

It takes me nine minutes to find the screwdriver.

Dad had moved everything around since Mom stopped doing things, and it was stuffed in a cupboard in the kitchen.

The whole time I'm thinking, be okay, be okay, be okay.

Because there was a time when she did something that wasn't okay.

It happened just before Dad left.

She did it with pills but she said it was an accident.

"I just needed to sleep," she said. "I just needed some sleep."

Dad and I sat with her at the hospital for two days.

Dad paced and paced and paced and I ate M&Ms.

When Mom woke up, she looked at him and said, "I just needed some sleep."

Dad swore.

Later, in the hallway, I heard the doctor say it would be better if Mom checked in somewhere.

"She needs around-the-clock care."

Dad said he understood, and he came in and told Mom. She just stared at the ceiling. He cleared his throat and his voice was shaky, but he said that he thought the doctor was right. "I can't do this, Roxie. I can't be here. And there's that ESPN thing. I have to go soon." It was his last chance. He said, "Mazzy can stay with Agnes. It won't be for long, hon. The doctor said it's best." I felt sick.

Mom's face was stone. "I just needed sleep," she whispered.

Later, when Dad went out to get some fresh air, Mom said this: "Mazzy, I'm going to talk to your dad, but you need to help me, okay? I don't want to go to a facility. I am not going to a facility."

"I don't want to live with Aunt Agnes," I said.

"You don't have to. We'll do this together. Do you understand?"

I didn't exactly but I said, "Yeah, Mom."

When Dad got back, Mom sat up and said, "Dave, Mazzy needs me. She just told me that she needs me and she doesn't want me to go. I'm not going to a treatment center."

Dad looked at me but Mom said, "She can hear this. She's a big girl."

He sighed and Mom went on. "We can hire someone to help around the house. We could even have Bill come. I'll go to therapy. Whatever. We can figure it out, but Mazzy needs me, and I need Mazzy." Her voice was clear.

Dad was shaking his head.

"I'm not going, Dave," she said, and sat up taller.

Dad leaned against the wall and let out a long breath.

"We can handle this. I just got tired. That's all." Her voice ran out.

Finally Dad looked up. "Roxie, I have to go to Connecticut. The job can't wait any longer and I can't leave the two of you alone."

"We'll be fine," Mom said. "Right, Maz?" She looked at me.

"Yeah, Dad," I said. "I'll take care of Mom. We'll be fine."

"See?" Mom said.

And Dad sighed again.

## TAKE CARE

That night Dad said he really wanted me to go to Kansas.

"I can't leave you and your mom alone."

"Dad, please. Please don't make me go."

He said if I didn't want to go to Kansas maybe he could find something else.

He said, "Couldn't you stay with one of your friends?"

Dad didn't get how nothing was the same anymore. He wasn't there. I just wanted to be with Mom. "No, Dad."

"What about summer camp?"

"No. I want to be home. We'll be fine."

He closed his eyes and I said, "I promise, Dad. It'll be okay."

That night I heard him on the phone with a whole bunch of nurses.

And then with Bill.

## PAINTING OLIVIA

I've tried to paint Olivia.

I've tried and tried.

I can't do it.

I can see her face but I can't paint it.

I wonder if she hates me.

NOT OLIVIA: oils on canvas

## STUPID

So far, Mom hasn't done anything stupid. She's stopped talking. She's stopped eating. She's stopped moving. She's stopped showering. She's stopped everything. But she hasn't done anything STUPID.

"Be okay, be okay," I say over and over while I look for the screwdriver. When I finally find it, I run to the bathroom, and just before I put it in the door, I say three more times, "Be okay, be okay, be okay," and do a yoga breath.


## COLBY

Colby comes home on his bike wobbling around because he has on cleats and football pants and a big bag on his back.

I say, "I didn't even know our school had a team."

"Yeah, duh."

"Oh," I say. "So did you make it?"

Colby wipes some sweat from his forehead. "Not yet," he says, and he comes and sits in the sprinklers with me. "I'm dead. Two-a-days are killing me."

"What are two-a-days?"

"Two practices in a day. I'd think you'd know that with your dad and everything."

"Oh," I say, and pull out a dandelion. "But you're not on the team?"

"Not yet."

I look at him. "Then why do you have to do two-a-days?"

He just shakes his head, which is lying in the wet grass, and then he opens his mouth so the water can get in.

Then I say how I might be a cheerleader.

He opens his eyes and says, "Yeah right."

"What?"

"You're not going to be a cheerleader."

"Why not?"

He closes his eyes again.

"Why not?" I say again.

"Because."

"Because why?"

He crosses his ankles and starts rubbing his stomach.

"Or I could be on the football team."

He laughs loud then. "Dream on," he said.

"I could. I could be an LB."

"An LB?" Now he flips over on his stomach and is looking at me. I pull out another dandelion and eat it.

"Sick."

"What?"

"You just ate a dandelion."

"I know."

"You are so weird."

"So?"

"So you are."

"So?"

"And you are not going to be an LB. You are way too little. Plus they don't even call them LBs. That sounds so dumb. You don't even know what you're talking about."

But I do.

And Colby probably knows I do, because of my dad and everything.

## DAD

Dad played football in college. His dream was to go to the NFL — the Steelers or the Bears.

But he tore his Achilles his senior year.

He tried to play after that but he was never really the same.

So then his dream was to work *Monday Night Football*. He almost has his dream.

I am going to ask Dad if calling a linebacker an LB sounds dumb.

DAD AS A FOOTBALL PLAYER: paint on canvas

## ME

I rattle the screwdriver but the door won't open.

There is no sound from the other side of the door.

I rattle some more. "Mom," I say, "please open the door."

Quiet.

"Mom, what are you doing in there? You told Dad you wouldn't do anything stupid."

Still quiet.

I rattle and rattle and rattle until finally the lock clicks and the door swings open.

The lights are glaring and her makeup is spread across the counter. Her brushes are out, her hair dryer, hair spray, gel, mask, almost every ounce of every bathroom product is crammed on the counter.

I look at the tub — the shower curtain is pulled.

"Mom?"

She doesn't answer but I do hear a sort of whimper.

I yank the curtain.

Her clothes are off and she is huddled in the corner of the empty jetted double tub.

"Mom?"

The whimpering gets a little louder and she just sits there.

"Mom?" I kneel down by the tub.

Her face is in her knees.

"Mom, it's okay. I can help you. Do you want me to help you?"

She doesn't say anything. I reach out to touch her shoulder and she moves away.

She is shivering and her shoulder blades stick out. Her skin looks like Elmer's glue.

I don't know what to do.

Until I think of what to do: I get her blanket.

Then I crawl in the tub and sit facing her.

She looks up. "What are you doing?" she whispers. Her lips are blue.

"I don't know," I say.

Mom just watches. And finally smiles.

I smile back.

We sit like that for a while.

And a while.

Until she suddenly says, "I can't do this."

Her face crumples and she is back in her knees.

"Do what, Mom?"

She sniffs and says even more quietly, "I can't be normal. I can't face Dave. I can't face anyone." She looks up at me. "And I can't be a mom."

I try to do three yoga breaths because for some reason I can't get air.

"Mom, don't say that. You're a good mom."

She is shaking now, and the Elmer's glue looks almost transparent.

"I let her die, Mazzy. I watched my own baby girl die." She is shaking harder now and I can feel tears coming up in my head but I don't want them to come. I don't want them to come. "I shouldn't be talking about this with you," she says. "I have no one to talk to." And then her voice trails off.

"Mom," I whisper. She is shaking and shaking and then sobbing. Sobbing so loud — louder than anything I've ever heard in my life and suddenly I'm shaking too.

"Mom," I whisper louder. "It wasn't your fault. It wasn't your fault."

Her head snaps up. "Then whose fault was it?" Her voice all of a sudden steady, her face a mess of snot and tears.

For some reason I feel scared. I'm scared.

"Nobody's," I say.

"What?" she says back.

"Nobody's."

"Mazzy, if it wasn't my fault, whose fault do you think it was?" she asks, her voice suddenly more than strong, almost a yell.

I take a deep breath.

Three deep breaths.

And then I say it.

I whisper it.

"Mazzy, I can't hear you." There is a tremor in the air. "What did you say?"

Finally, I look straight at her and say what we both know is the truth. What Dad knows is the truth. What probably the whole neighborhood and the cops and the paramedics and everybody know is the truth. "Mine, Mom. I said it was my fault."


## HOT

The day Olivia died it was hot outside just like now.

Sweaty hot.

And it was 9:43. My first gymnastics class ever started at 10:00 and it was in Springville, which was a half hour away.

For two weeks I had put up signs: Gymnastics 10:00 Saturday, August 4th, Springville Center.

I put them up in the kitchen, in my parents bathroom, on the fridge, on my dad's steering wheel. Everywhere.

It was because I saw this flyer at the grocery store for Xtreme Gymnastics and I wanted to do it and I got all my friends to sign up and it was going to be perfect.

But sometimes things didn't always happen how they were supposed to. Dad said, "Mazzy, you've papered the whole house," and then he laughed. "You'd think this was the most important gymnastics class on the planet."

I karate chopped at him and said, "I just don't want to miss it."

"Yeah. I get it." He laughed again. And he karate chopped back.

But then the day of the class he was called in to work.

And Mom was mad because she had art critiques and didn't have time and she'd have to take Olivia with her and she didn't have time for this and why did Dad always do this. I was sitting by the door waiting and Mom was rushing around and I said, "You can just drop me off early and come back," but she said, "I don't have time, Maz. I have to get to the art center by 10:30," and then she was getting in the shower but it was 9:15 and she wouldn't be ready in time.

I didn't want to go if I was going to be late. I could feel the heat rising in my throat.

"Mom, I don't want to go," I said.

But she wasn't listening. She was yelling to get everything ready, to get Olivia wiped up, and she was putting on her makeup and she was almost ready, she said, and I was still standing by the door waiting and waiting and waiting.

Then it was 9:49 and I said, "I'll just stay home."

Mom poked her head in the hall. "You are not staying home." Olivia was sitting on the floor.

Finally she came out of her room with bags and some books and her art portfolio and hurry hurry we're late, get your sister and let's go. The phone rang. Her cell rang. Olivia started crying. Hurry Hurry. This is costing us a fortune, Mazzy, and we're late.

I picked up Olivia.

I picked up my bag.

Mom was on the phone and she motioned to go out to the car.

Outside.

I went outside.

Me and Olivia were outside.

I opened the Range Rover door and a burst of hot air hit my face.

Too hot.

I put Olivia down on the grass. She crawled around. I put my bag on the ground.

I wanted to cry.

I didn't want to go. I didn't want to walk in late. Mom was still inside. I felt sweat start on my forehead. I looked over at Colby's. Everything was still. The whole neighborhood was still on a Saturday morning at 9:52. Why wasn't Mom out here? Why did it never work? Mom was too busy to take me. Dad was too busy. I didn't want to go. I got in the car. It was so hot. It was so hot and the sweat was trickling down my back.

Finally she came out.

10:01.

Finally she got in the car.

10:02.

She was still on her cell phone.

She smiled at me.

I ignored her.

She turned on the car.

10:03.

The sweat made it down to my butt.

She backed up fast.

She backed up so fast.

Too fast.

So fast.

She backed up.

And

we heard it.

A bump.

Mom said, "What was that?"

I said, "I don't know."

Mom looked back at me, and her face went white. "Why isn't Olivia in her seat?"

I looked over.

Olivia was not in her seat.

Olivia was not in her seat.

Olivia was not in her seat.

Olivia died at 10:04 on Saturday, August 4th.

I still have the gymnastics flyer.


## BLACK AND WHITE

After I say "It was my fault," Mom puts her head back on her knees and sobs.

I just look at the tile on the wall.

Black tiles brown tiles white tiles. Black brown white black brown white black brown white.

Mom doesn't say anything black brown white black brown white.

She just sobs and shakes and sobs and shakes and black brown white black brown.

"Mazzy," she finally whispers.

Black brown white black brown white. "Mazzy." Her voice in a tunnel.

Black brown white black brown white. "Mazzy, look at me."

Black brown white — "Mazzy" — she is grabbing my arms.

"Mazzy, it wasn't your fault."

Brown.

"It wasn't your fault."

Black.

"Did you hear me?"

Brown.

"Did you hear me, baby girl?"

White.

"Did you hear me?" A hand on my arm.

Black.

"Mazzy."

Brown.

Arms around me. My mom's arms the first time in a year.

White.

"It wasn't your fault."

Black.

"It wasn't your fault."

White.

I put my head on her shoulder.

## ARTICLES

Dad collected articles after it happened.

Articles about other incidents. "It's not that uncommon," he'd say. Like that would make it better.

He'd put them on the fridge. "It happens all the time. Five kids were killed in Iowa. Separate incidents. All involving backing up."

Then Mom stopped coming into the kitchen.

And he stopped bringing them home.


## TUB

Mom and I sit in the tub for a long time.

So long that she starts shaking because she doesn't have any clothes on and the blanket I brought is thin.

"Hang on," I say.

I get her robe and three more quilts and pillows and a bag of chips.

I also bring a new sorbet and two spoons and the noni just in case.

"What are you doing?" she whispers.

"Getting this stuff."

"I can see that," she says, and then we are sitting in blankets and the sleeping bag and eating sorbet in the big jetted tub.

At first we just sit there.

But then I start telling her stuff. Normal stuff. Stuff she usually ignores.

I say, "I think Colby shaves."

She smiles, so I keep talking.

"I think it's weird," I say. "He always has these pieces of toilet paper on his face that are bloody and he also says he's only attracted to vampires."

She laughs and says, "What?"

"He's only attracted to vampires."

"Oh," she says, "he likes you."

"He does? How do you know?"

"Because that's what boys say when they like girls."

"Oh," I say.

Mom drinks some of the noni and she doesn't even look like it's gross.

We sit and sit and then she says something. She says, "I'm not going to teach art lessons anymore."

She says it quiet and I'm not sure if I heard her right.

"I'm going to do something else."

"Like what?"

"I don't know. Maybe just do art."

"And not teach?"

"Not for a while."

"I think that's okay."

"You do?" She looks at me.

"Uh huh."

Then I say, "I got out your paintings."

Mom is scraping her sorbet bowl and she doesn't look mad, so I say,

"I got out your paintings and I've been doing stuff in your studio."

I pause. She licks her spoon.

"Are you mad?"

"Mad? Why would I be mad?"

"No reason," I say.

Then I take a bite of my sorbet.

Then I tell her this:

"I want an Oprah bra."

"Why?"

"Because I hate my boobs and Oprah has this bra training that helps you pick out the right bra for your body and I want a bra that pushes my boobs together."

"Why?"

"Because they're so small."

"Baby, they'll get bigger."

"When?"

"I don't know but they'll get there."

"How big?"

"Pretty big. Look at how big mine are."

She shows me and they are bigger than I thought they'd be.

"They'll get like those?"

"Probably."

"But you don't know when."

"Nope."

"So I can't get the bra?"

She blows out some air and says, "How long have I been asleep?"

"A long time," I say.

"We'll get you the bra."

Then she tells me this:

"I like the noni juice."

I don't say anything because that makes me think of Norma.

"What's wrong?"

"Nothing."

"Nothing?"

"Well, Norma's sick and she didn't tell me." And then I tell her what happened.

"Huh," says Mom.

"What?" I say.

"I'd like to talk to Norma," she says.

"Me too," I say.


Then I tell her this:

"And her dad is dead."

"Whose dad?"

"Norma's."

"Oh," Mom says.

"But she still talks to him."

She doesn't say anything.

"Do you ever talk to Olivia?"

Mom closes her eyes.

Then she tells me this:

"I might tell Dad that I want another baby."

"Really?"

"Maybe two or three."

"Really?"

"What do you think he'll say?"

"I don't know."

"Do you think it's a good idea?"

"I don't know."

"I know," she says.

And then we sit.

"Would you have another operation?"

"I don't know. No."

"Oh."

"I don't know. I don't know what I'm talking about."

"Okay."

"Do you think it's a good idea?"

"Yeah."

"You do?"

"I don't know," I say.

"Okay," she says.

Mom falls asleep first and I watch her chest go in and out and in and out.

I fall asleep second and I think about my chest going in and out.

She's back.

## OPRAH

If we got on *Oprah* we could tell our story.

Me and Mom.

## FACE

There is a face, Dad's, and he is staring at us.

"What's going on?"

I wipe my eyes and try to focus.

"What are you two doing in here?"

Mom is still asleep.

"Get out of there, Mazzy. What is going on?"

"Nothing."

"Why are you in the bathtub?"

"What?"

"Why are you two sleeping in the bathtub? Why are there signs on the doors outside? There's a huge stain on the carpet and the house is a mess. The room is a mess."

Dad's face is red and his hair doesn't look how it usually does.

"Dad, it's fine. Everything is fine." And it really is. Mom is back and she isn't going to teach and they are going to have more babies. And I am going to be a big sister. Everything is fine.

But he doesn't say, "Oh good. Everything is okay." Instead he says, "Roxie."

Mom doesn't move. I look at her. She looks so peaceful.

"Roxie," he says again. Nothing.

He doesn't move to touch her or anything. He just gets louder.

"ROXIE."

His voice makes me feel sick. I want to say, "Leave her alone. She's okay. Leave her alone."

But Dad's face is red and he is clenched and I don't dare say anything.

Instead I shake Mom's shoulder.

Mom's eyes slowly start to open. "Mom," I whisper. "Mom, it's okay. Everything's okay."

She looks dazed.

"What's going on, Roxie?" he says.

She looks at him.

He says it louder. "What the hell is going on?"

I want to hit him. I want to hit him so hard. Everything is okay, Dad. Stop it.

Everything is okay.

I look at Mom.

And then I see it happen.

I see it happen. Her eyes start to thicken and her breathing gets deeper and then Mom goes back to bed.

## DIABETES

When you have diabetes you have problems with your blood sugar.

You can get it when you're little or when you're old or fat.

You can die from it.

You can get your toes cut off from it.

You can go blind from it.

## NORMA

Norma comes over while I'm in the sprinklers.

Dad is inside trying to "fix things."

Norma says, "How are you?"

I say nothing.

"Mazzy, I can tell you're upset at me, but can we talk about it?"

I pull a dandelion up and smell it. Good.

Norma stands there and I sit there and her slippers are getting wet.

Big fluffy pink slippers that are brown all around the bottom and now soaking wet.

"Your slippers," I say.

She looks down. "Yep," she says.

And then we are both looking at them.

"Your dad home?"

"Uh-huh."

"That good or bad?"

"I don't know," I say, and pick another dandelion.

"Oh."

"So I don't need your help anymore."

"You don't?"

"No."

"Not at all?"

"Nope."

She pulls a foot out of the sopping slipper and scratches her bulby leg with her toe.

"I still need your help with the weeds, though."

"Can't."

"Can't?"

"Nope."

"Okay."

"Okay."

And then she walks away but she leaves one of her pink sopping slippers right there in the sprinkler.

I don't say anything.

I might cut it up.

NORMA'S SLIPPER: chalk on cement

## OLIVIA

Sometimes, not all the time, but sometimes, I want to grab Olivia and shake her.

I want to say, LOOK WHAT YOU DID TO MOM. LOOK WHAT YOU DID TO DAD. LOOK WHAT YOU DID TO ME.

LOOK.

LOOK.

LOOK.

I want her to have never been born.

And then, when I think that, when I want that, I sit in the sprinklers and I am a bad person.

## PROFESSIONAL HELP

When I come inside I hear Dad say, "She doesn't want that."

I hold the door so it won't close loud and it doesn't even click.

He is on the phone.

"I don't know," he says. "Maybe I could quit and take care of her. It's my fault things got this bad."

Who is he talking to?

Dad swears and my throat tightens. "Yes, I realize she needs professional help." Professional help.

He is going to put her somewhere.

I tiptoe the other way, into Mom's bedroom.

She has to be better. She has to be like last night.

The lights are out and it's so dark. Too dark.

I flip them on and there she is.

Back in bed.

With her blue nightgown and her glue face and her eyes closed.

She almost looks dead.

"Mom," I whisper.

Nothing.

"Mom?" I stand by her bed and look at her face. She is breathing. "Mom? Mom, wake up." I put my hand on her mouth; she doesn't move.

I put my hand on her mouth and her nose.

She moves.

She grunts and rolls to her side.

"Mom. Please wake up," I say.

Her body goes up and down.

"Mom? Please?"

I look at her body up and down, up and down.

"Mom? You have to wake up. Dad is going to put you somewhere."

Up and down.

"Mom. Mom? Listen to me."

Up and down.

"Mom!"

I can feel it rising in me. Why won't she just wake up? Why won't she just be normal? Wake up. Wake up. Wake up.

"Mom, you don't want to go to a facility. Remember? You said to help you. You said to help you and take care of you." My eyes are blurring with tears but she doesn't respond.

So I say it. I yell it: "Mom. Olivia is dead."

Up and down.

"She's dead."

Up and down.

"And I'm not and it's not my fault and it's not your fault. It's nobody's fault. Remember? We decided. And you want another baby. Remember?"

Up and down.

"Mom, wake up. Please, wake up."

Up and down.

"Dad is going to take you away. Mom, please?"

Up and down.

"Please, Mom. Please don't do this." And I start to shake her how I want to shake Olivia. I start to shake them both. Please don't do this. Please.

Please.

Please.

Please.

PLEASE!

That's when Dad comes in.

That's when Dad comes in and hugs me and I am all wet and soggy and please don't do this MOM.

## SIT DOWN

Dad says, "Sit down."

I sit down.

"Baby," he says, but I'm not his baby. "Baby, we've made a decision."

We. We. Him.

"We've decided that your mother should spend some time at a facility that can help her get better."

I close my eyes.

"I know you aren't happy with this decision, but what's important is getting your mom better."

Inside my eyes I can see light from the window.

"I love you and your mother a great deal."

I hear a buzzing and I wonder if someone has left the cable box on.

"Do you hear me, Maz? I love both of you."

I wish no one would touch the cable box.

"Maz?"

I nod.

"I love you both and I want what's best for you."

I think about Colby and his football pads.

"So your mother is going to go to the Park Facility. I've called and they are expecting us in tomorrow."

I take a yoga breath and then I think, Do you buy your own football pads or does the school loan them out?

"Did you hear me, Maz? We're taking your mother there in the morning so we need to get her all ready."

That's when I have my idea.

"Dad?" I say.

"Yes."

"Do you still have your football pads?"

He looks perplexed. "Why, honey? Do you want to hit something?"

"No."

"Then why do you want the pads?"

"Because."

He folds his arms and sits back on the couch. "I still have some pads in the cold storage. You can do whatever you want with them."

"Thanks," I say, and I stand up.

"We're not done, Mazzy."

"What?"

"Sit down."

"Why?"

"Sit down."

"I have to go."

"You can listen for a few more minutes."

Then he starts talking football talk. He says that sometimes you want to make the perfect pass. You want to win the game but the defense keeps breaking down and you get sacked over and over.

"No one wants to get sacked, Mazzy. Do you understand?"

I pull a string out of my collar.

"I never anticipated getting sacked. Not like this — not over and over."

I tie the string around my pinky.

"But sometimes," he says, "after so many setbacks, after interceptions and penalties and all kinds of things, sometimes you have to just go back to the drawing board. You have to start over."

I tie it too tight and my finger starts to go red.

"Maz? Are you listening to me?"

It is getting redder.

"Maz. Look at me."

I pull harder.

"Maz. Look. At. Me." His voice is loud.

I look at him.

"Your mom is going to the hospital."

"You already told me that."

"Let me finish," he says. "Your mom is going to the hospital and I have been doing well at this new job."

He stops talking. I am pulling on the string.

"I have been doing well and they want me to cover some big events, but there's going to be a lot of travel."

The string pops.

"So your mom is going to the hospital and you are going to stay with your aunt in Kansas."

## PIGS

On *Oprah*, you can buy a pig or a goat or a sheep.

But you don't get to keep it.

They give it to starving people in Africa.

You can even buy half a pig.

I want half a pig.

I'm going to ask Mom if I can buy half a pig to give to starving people in Africa.

Or I might ask Norma.

Or Dixie.

Dixie would want to help too.

I won't ask Dad. I'll never ask Dad anything ever again.

ME AND DIXIE AND HALF A PIG: oil on canvas

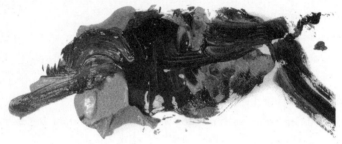

## KANSAS

My dad thinks I'm going to live in Kansas and my mom is going to a treatment center.

I find the football pads.

I find some cleats.

I find some old jerseys.

They are all in a box and I pull them out of the closet while doing yoga breaths.

Dad is in the kitchen on his cell when he sees me with the box and he says, "Hang on a minute" into the phone and then says to me, "What're you doing, Maz?"

"Nothing."

He looks at me.

"Can we talk?"

I start pulling the box across the tile.

"Maz?"

I pull it to the carport door and then I turn and look at him.

"Maz? This isn't permanent."

Not permanent. Lie.

I close my eyes and do three karate chops at him. Hard. Fast. And then I go out the door.

## FOOTBALL PADS

I go behind the Spyder and put on the pads and one of the jerseys and the cleats.

Then I go and sit in the Dean Machine.

I could get in trouble but I don't care.

Dad is watching from the window, I'm sure.

Probably everyone is watching.

I hope that Colby is watching.

I am in the Dean Machine for six minutes when Norma comes out.

"What's going on?" Norma is standing by the side of the boat.

"Nothing."

"Nothing?"

"Nope."

She has purple lipstick on but I don't care.

"I like your football clothes."

"It's a uniform."

"Oh."

"I'm going to be an LB on the team."

"An LB?"

"Uh-huh."

"What's an LB?"

"A linebacker."

"Huh. I've never heard anyone call a linebacker an LB."

I do a yoga breath. "You probably don't know anything about football."

I won't look at her but I can feel her trying to be friends again.

"Nope, I don't."

"I do."

She is quiet.

I pretend like I am turning the wheel of the boat. Colby says it's easy to drive. Easy to drive the Dean Machine and probably easy to drive the Spyder.

"Mazzy," she says all quiet, "Mazzy . . . I'm going to try to explain one more time. After that it's up to you."

I wish I had the key to the Dean Machine.

"I have bad health and I've been trying to get better."

"So," I say.

"So, I eat too much."

"Yeah. I can see that." I am being mean. She clears her throat and is about to say something when I say, "It doesn't matter."

"What do you mean?"

"It doesn't matter," I say again. And it's true.

"Okay." She wipes some sweat from her neck. "So, can we be friends again?"

"Not right now." She doesn't know that we can never be friends because I'm leaving.

"Okay. Later?"

"Maybe."

That's when a door slams and it's Colby.

## BELLY BUTTONS

When ladies get pregnant, their belly buttons stick out. Even if they were innies before, they go out after a while.

And the skin looks like elephants.

Mom and me, we'd look at her belly button and I'd try to poke it back in.

"Maz, it won't go back until the baby's here."

"Oh," I said. "Can I color it?"

"Okay," she said.

I got the markers and I made a ladybug on her belly button.

## PLAN

"What are you doing in the Dean Machine?" Colby is wearing his swim-suit again.

"I'm sitting in it."

Norma is still standing there and Colby is climbing onto the boat. "Move over," he says.

I move to the passenger seat.

"You can only come on here if I say."

"Okay."

Norma still stands and Colby doesn't even look at her or say anything to her. Then he says, "Where'd you get those pads?"

"The team."

"What team?"

"The football team."

"What football team?"

"The Florida Gators."

"That's a real jersey from the Gators?"

"Yeah. It's my dad's," I say, and Colby bites his lip.

"Oh," he says.

We keep sitting there and Norma keeps standing there until she finally turns around and goes back to her house.

I want to say, "Bye Norma," but I don't.

"She's weird," Colby says.

"Yeah," I say. "But I like her."

Then he says, "I saw your dad."

"Yeah."

"He's home?"

"Yeah."

Colby flips a switch on the boat.

"Are you glad?"

"No."

"Why not?"

"Because."

Then I say, "Colby? Do you like these pads and jersey and stuff?"

"No," he says, and he is doing something under the steering wheel.

"Oh," I say. "But do you want them?"

He looks at me. "What do you mean?"

"I could give them to you. And the cleats and the jersey. My dad said I could do whatever I wanted with them."

"Why?"

"Why did my dad say that or why would I give them to you?"

"The give them to me part."

I take a deep breath. This has to sound good. "I'll give them to you if you do something for me."

"What?"

I look back at the house. No Dad. Norma is inside.

Then I say very quietly, "Steal the Spyder."

"What?"

"Steal the Spyder."

COLBY AND MAZZY IN DEAN MACHINE: crayon on paper

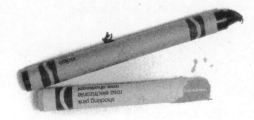

## PLANS

Oprah says: you gotta plan.

And on *Survivor* you make plans.

No one knew until I talked to Colby that I had a plan.

## DINNER

Dad takes me to dinner that night.

Dad calls Bill to come over and watch Mom while we are gone.

Mom is home alone all the time. He doesn't need to call Bill.

Brick oven pizza.

He tries to talk to me. "So, what's your summer been like? We never got to really talk on the phone."

I pull a pepperoni off and put it in my lemonade.

"Nothing," I say.

"Nothing?"

"Nope."

"Didn't you go to the lake with the Deans a few times?"

I look at him. How does he know that?

"No."

"You didn't?"

"No."

"Mazzy, I know you did. I talked to Ellen."

Mrs. Dean.

"She said she took you to yoga and shopping and you had a great time."

"We didn't."

"You didn't what?"

"We didn't have a great time. I hated it and Mom was mad that Mrs. Dean made me go."

Dad sighs. He sighs like he is some authority on my life or yoga and shopping with Mrs. Dean.

I decide to give him one chance. One more chance.

"Dad," I say, "can't you just let Mom stay home?"

He picks up his Coke. "I can't, Maz," he says, and takes a long drink. "Your mother is sick."

"Well, can I at least come with you to Connecticut? I don't want to go to Kansas. Please, Dad."

Another long drink, and then he shakes his head and says, "Not now. Soon. When I get settled."

"Fine," I say, and I don't say one more word the rest of the dinner.

He asked for it.


## WHEN WE GET HOME

Dad goes into his office and I stand there.

Finally I yell, "I'm sleeping in Mom's room."

Dad says from his office, "Not a good idea, Mazzy. I'm staying with your mom."

I yell it again. "I'm sleeping in Mom's room."

Dad comes out of his office and says, "Honey, I'm going to sit up with your mother. I haven't seen her for weeks."

"That's not my fault. I want to sleep in her room."

I walk out of the room, down the hall, and lock myself in her room.

I put my face to the door for ten seconds.

Nobody comes so I get started.

## CLOTHES

I pick out her painting jeans, a white button-down, and blue earrings.
The ones she wore to my elementary school graduation.

I find her old Tevas so she would be comfortable and I lay them all out
on her bed.

I don't even try to talk to her.

Then I pull out her suitcase and throw stuff in. Her umbrella, her wind-
breaker, her walking shoes, her maps, her wallet — especially her wallet
with credit cards.

After I have everything in and ready, I try to get her in the jeans.

"Mom?"

She doesn't reply.

I sit her up and try to pull her nightgown up. She turns away and lies
back down.

"Mom? I'm trying to help you."

She goes into a ball.

"Mom. They are taking you away so we have to leave tonight. I know you
can hear me. If you want to go, and I know you want to go, look at me."

She doesn't.

"Just look at me once and I'll know you want to go."

She doesn't.

But she is probably just tired.

It takes me over an hour to get her dressed.

Usually she'd be limp and I could change her. This time she is stiff.

I even put her Tevas on her so we'd be all ready, and then I pull the covers over her just in case.

It is 10:13 and I haven't heard anything from Dad.

At 10:54 Dad knocks on the door.

I am lying on the bed watching the clock — I don't answer the door.

He knocks again. "Mazzy, can I come in?"

I pull the sheet up to Mom's chin and say, "No."

"Mazzy, let me in."

I hide the suitcases — hers and mine — and open the door.

"Baby," he says, "I want you to sleep in your own room. You need a good night's sleep."

"I don't want to."

"Come on, Mazzy. You need to sleep in your own bed and let your mom get some rest."

He looks over my shoulder at her. Even how she is, her face white and sunken, even like that she is still beautiful. His eyes start to fill up. If he loves her so much, why is he making her go to a facility?

"Mom is used to me in here. I always sleep here," I say. It isn't all the way true but sometimes.

"She's sick, Maz. And this is her last night at home."

I lean against the door. "If I don't sleep in here, then you can't sleep in here, either."

He closes his eyes for a long time and then says, "I won't."

"You won't?"

"No."

"Where are you going to sleep?"

"In the study."

145

The study. Three doors down. Beyond my room.

"Okay," I say.

"Okay?"

"Okay."

"And then tomorrow morning we'll all go together and you'll see that the place where your mom will be staying is nice."

He swallows. "Really nice and she'll get better."

He is staring at her.

Dad in the study will make the plan easier.

I take his hand. "Okay, Dad." I say. "Will you tuck me in?"

He smiles at me like I really want him to tuck me in.

I don't.

"Okay," he says. "Okay, honey."

And then we leave but I look back at Mom and send her a mental message: 1:00 a.m.


When Dad comes to tuck me in he tries to talk to me.

He keeps trying to say things.

Over and over and over.


## FINE

I don't go to sleep.

Instead, in my mind I try to work it out better.

It is going to work.

She will be okay. We can do it. She is fine.

Me waiting: pencil on notebook paper

At 12:45 I get out of bed.

## EVERYTHING

At 12:52 I am dressed and ready to go.

I have the keys in my pocket.

12:54 I am in Mom's room and she is exactly how I left her. In a ball with Tevas on.

"Okay, Mom. Wake up. It's now." I shake her.

She doesn't move. I don't really expect her to move but I think maybe. Or maybe not.

"It's okay," I say. "I've got help."

Then I open her window and throw our suitcases into the bushes.

"The suitcases are outside," I say. Still in a ball. "I'm going to go get everything ready and then I'll be back." Balled.

As I climb out the window, I feel a rush of something go through me.

This is going to work — because everything is going to be different from now on.

Everything.

## BEACHY HEAD

Colby is sitting in the Spyder.

He is wearing a black hoodie, black jeans, and had black something smeared all over his face.

"What's that?" I ask as I put the suitcases in the backseat.

"Shhh," he says. "What's what?"

"The stuff on your face." He is gripping the steering wheel.

"Blackout for football."

"Why's it on your face?"

"Duh," he says. And then: "Where's your mom?"

"She's coming. But I might need your help."

"For what?"

"To get her."

Colby stares at me and I say, "Hang on. I'll be right back. You probably won't have to do anything."

I go back to the window and climb into Mom's room. She is in the same position.

I pull off the cover. "It's time to go, Mom."

She doesn't move.

"Mom, we're leaving now." I pull her to a seated position but she is resisting. "You have to help me, Mom, because we have to go out the window." She won't get up.

"Please, Mom. Please get up. You have to help me."

I try to pull her up but she is almost pulling the other way. She just doesn't get it. She wouldn't want to go to the facility. She would want to leave with me.

"Come on, Mom. We're going in the Spyder. You'll feel the wind and then we can go to Beachy Head. We're going to go to Beachy Head." Still resisting.

I sit by her and look at her face. Closed. Smooth. White. "I'll take care of you, Mom. Don't worry. I'll get you out of here and you'll feel better once we're in the car."

Her mouth sort of moves.

"I saw that, Mom. I saw that. Once you feel the wind in the Spyder, you'll, you'll feel better. And we can go to the airport and fly to Beachy Head."

Her mouth moves again and I know she wants to go. I know she does but she just can't get up by herself.

"Wait, Mom. I'll get help. Wait right here," I say, and then I climb through the window to get Colby.

When my mom feels the wind, she will wake up. She'll be okay. She won't go to the hospital and I won't go to Kansas.

## HELP

"Come on," I whisper.

"Where?"

"To get my mom."

"I thought you just went to get her."

"I did."

"Then where is she?"

"I need your help to get her out the window."

"What? Like carry her? I'm not carrying your mom."

He is whispering too loud.

"You don't have to carry her. Just help her."

"I thought she wanted to go. I thought this was her idea."

I can tell he is getting nervous, but he can't back out. I need him.

We argue for ten more minutes until finally I say, "It's okay. I'll get her by myself."

I turn to leave, but he opens the car door and gets out.

"Fine, I'll help. But this is getting weirder and weirder, and if I get in trouble I won't talk to you again."

"Okay."

"Okay."


When we get to her room — Colby and I through the window — she is gone.

The bed is empty.

Yoga breath. Yoga breath.

"Where is she?" Colby asks.

"Shh," I say. Yoga breath. "Shh. She's here. She's just doing something really quick."

I look on the other side of the bed.

"What are you doing?" he whispers.

I look under the bed.

"You think your mom is under the bed?" Colby says.

Yoga breath.

"No. I'm just seeing if I left my bag."

I look in the bathroom.

Nothing.

She is gone.

## SILENCE

"Maybe she's already outside," I say.

"Whatever," Colby says. "We have to go. This is taking way too long."

We climb back out and look around. No mom.

"Wait here," I tell him.

"I'm going home."

"No, no, please," I say. "Just wait here."

I go back inside.

Everything is still.

In the front room, the clock is ticking.

In the kitchen, the fridge is buzzing.

I look in my room.

Nothing.

I look in the hall closet.

Nothing.

I look in the bathroom.

Nothing.

I even open the door of the study a crack.

That's when I hear it.

## TALKING

At the end of the hall. In the art studio.

My dad's voice.

I tiptoe down the hall and put my ear to the door.

He is talking.

But not with his TV voice.

And not his dad voice.

It's different.

I open the door quietly and there they are.

In the moonlight streaming through the window.

Dad on the rocking chair.

Mom in his lap.

Dad whispering and talking.

## OPRAH

If I meet her I'll say that she was wrong about some things.

## PAINTINGS

I stand in the doorway and watch them. Dad has all my paintings out on the floor.

Mom is just curled up — her Tevas dangling.

"I'm sorry," he says. "I am so sorry. I am so sorry. I miss Olivia so much, but I miss both of you too."

I stand there.

And watch him cry and then I see her put her arms around him and hug him.

My mom hugs my dad.

They sit like that a long time.

Rocking.

Then I hear Dad say, "I didn't know Mazzy could paint."

I hold my breath.

She doesn't respond right away but then she says, "She can."

I let the air out and that's when I close the door.

## WENDY'S

Instead of kidnapping my mom, Colby and I go to Wendy's for two free Frosties.

We walk.

## MORNING

In the morning, Mom is sitting in the front room.

She has two suitcases and she is wearing the same outfit I put her in.

She looks like Mom.

Dad is making a power shake in the kitchen and he doesn't say anything about her clothes.

As we are leaving and getting in Dad's car, Norma comes over.

She is in a fluorescent muumuu and she has her hair in curlers.

"You all need any help?" she asks.

I look at Dad.

He looks at me.

"I think we do, actually," he says.


OLIVIA: watercolor on paper

The END.